GUTSY'S LUCK

GUTSY'S LUCK

Rhea M. Coleman

First Edition

Printed in the United States of America

Library of Congress Cataloging in Publication Data:
Coleman, Rhea M., 1924-
Gutsy's luck / by Rhea M. Coleman.—1st ed.
p. cm.
Summary: Relates a young boy's adventures as he follows a mule train down the Santa Fe Trail from Kansas City.
ISBN: 0-86534-187-7: $12.95
[1. Santa Fe Trail—Fiction. 2. Adventure and adventurers—Fiction. 3. West (U.S.)—Fiction.] I.Title.
PZ7.C67724Gu 1993
[Fic]—dc20 92-21773
CIP
AC

Published by SUNSTONE PRESS
Post Office Box 2321
Santa Fe, NM 87504-2321 / USA

Dedicated to
Nicole, Eric, Alex, Curtis,
Rhea, Crystal, Victoria,
Sara and Matthew.

Appreciation to
Helen Barton, Constance A. Guy
and Marrie Ewing.
They believed.

Hiding place for many. Garden of the Gods — *Burton G. Vose*

ONE

Little Cerrillos Hills

Jeb squirmed and twisted in his saddle. Things seemed all right. But, if things were okay, why was he so itchy? Maybe that trouble at the saddler's was still stuck in his craw.

By gum, he would never buy another mule fitting from that ornery critter. The kid was only being curious. No reason for him to be so terrified, unless old Barnes was as mean as the men said. Jeb hoped the kid was safe. He noticed no one, 'cept old Barnes, hunted very hard. Looked as if they were afraid they might find the kid. People like old Barnes made Jeb glad to be a mule skinner.

"Come on, Cookie, move it! Wake old Bess up. Make her bell jangle. A good run will get those city cramps outta' all of us," shouted Jeb.

It was good to leave that city behind. No need now to be afraid to let out a good whoop. No need to be careful when he hopped on a mule. They were not city chairs that might break. Those old mules were used to yelling, cussing, clapping and prodding.

Why, this morning Jeb could hardly make those mules start for fear he would offend a city dandy. He could not imagine how one thousand people could be content, gathered together in one place with no elbow room for anybody. *Gad! I feel sorry for them,* thought Jeb.

"Shake it up, Cookie, put a little heat on that slow-moving critter. Let's make some time today. I got a hankering for air that somebody else ain't breathed before," said Jeb.

Cookie whacked old Bess. As her bell rang faster the mules of the train picked up the pace.

"Now, now, my good man," called Bible John, "we've lots of time and the Good Book says we must treat our animals as brothers."

"Glad to know that," hollered Jeb, "'cause now I know what to do to my brother if he ever acts as lazy as those good-for-nothing beasts."

"When will we be stopping?" asked Doc, gasping as he bounced along in his saddle.

"There's a special place up ahead where there's plenty of water and good long grass. If we keep up this pace we should make it early enough to set up camp during the daylight," Jeb answered.

"Oh," moaned Doc, as he grasped his saddle horn to keep himself steady. "I'm not accustomed to long rides. I'll admit I hoped for a slow first few days so I would have more time to adjust to the saddle."

Along the Turqoise trail. *Burton G. Vose*

TWO

Gosi had never followed a mule train before, to come right down to it he had not spent much time in the woods. He did not realize that Rocky, the rear scout, would keep doubling back to make sure nothing could surprise the team from that direction. Nor did he know that Flatnose was an old-time trapper who from years of living alone in the wilderness, could not stay bunched up with train, but would roam freely, reading trail signs and helping the scouts.

Gosi did not know that his own signs of travel and those of the train would show very differently to the scouts. The truth was, Gosi knew frontier life, but for real scouting and trailing, his entire experiences had been in his dreams. He was a real greenhorn. After he had been on the trail a while he looked back and realized he had started out as green as any tenderfoot from New York City or Philadelphia.

On this, his first day, he thought only of his colossal good luck. He had supreme confidence that, to quote an old saying his paw used, he had "a bear by the tail on a downhill drag."

He climbed back up the tree to watch. He listened to the rhythm of the bell; he was sure he could easily outrun the heavily laden animals. He listened joyfully to the noise of Cookie's pots, clamoring and banging. He could hear the creaking of the saddles and the packs. Here, he figured, he could be of help; he knew how to care for saddles and packs.

First, he must let the train get far enough away from Westport so there would be no way to make him go back. If he got a chance to prove how much he could help them, he was sure they would let him travel along. Maybe they would let him eat with them, too. Thinking of food make Gosi's stomach cramp. He climbed down the tree and ate some of the hickory nuts, cracking them against a rock.

He planned the rest of his day. First, he would sleep so he could stay awake all night. Until now Gosi had always gone to bed when it got dark; but this was a new life, and he expected it to be different. After he got up he must eat and drink before he followed the tracks of the train.

Simple. No problem, thought Gosi, when he had crawled back into his cave. After a time of twisting and turning, though, he saw that he did have one little problem. He could not get to sleep. Perhaps it was the excitement; perhaps it was the long sleep of the afternoon and night before. The cause did not matter; Gosi could not sleep.

Next, in his wakefulness, he thought how he had eaten all the berries close by the cave. This meant he had to move away from the area to find more.

Third, with all the noise the loaded mules made, he would never find another squirrel's cache. He had better fill his pockets again from this one. At least he knew where a ready supply was stored.

Fourth, time crawled. He would just have to get moving. He crawled out of the cave. He went to the stream and drank some water. He decided he could risk bathing; after all, he might not have another opportunity, and it would give him something to do.

He revisited the squirrel's cache of nuts. As he dug into the hole they came cascading down and scattered far and wide.

"Well," said Gosi to any squirrel that might be near, "looks like you have really packed this tree. Wouldn't you know that I'd start from the bottom. Here, I'll block this hole up with some sticks and stones so all your food won't slide out and be wasted."

After finishing his repair job, he filled his pockets. He was happy to see the sun was high in the sky; that meant he could have lunch. Afterwards, he threw a few rocks and kicked a few pebbles. He climbed the tree; he climbed down; he drank more water; he picked more berries. Still the sun had barely started down into the western horizon.

Gosi decided to travel a little way down the trail. If there was any disturbance, he could hide. He walked a little and listened. He ran a little and sat down to wait for time to pass to make up for the running. He realized he was so happy he was whistling.

He stopped whistling and tried counting slowly and quietly. He took two steps forward and one back. Finally, he sat down and listened for any noise that might give him clues as to how far ahead the train was by now.

Startled, he heard the sound of a horse galloping toward him. Gosi left the trail quickly and hid under a clump of bushes. He listened carefully, but now the only sound beside the hoofbeats was that of Gosi's thumping heart. He wasn't sure which was louder. Gosi held his breath.

Rocky dismounted and walked the trail, examining the tracks left by Gosi's moccasin-type shoes. Slowly, he remounted his horse and followed the tracks back to the place where Gosi had crossed the stream.

Rocky whispered to Crown, his horse, "Wait here. Nope, you'd better come along; I'd hate to see some Injun brave ride off with ye and me have to walk."

Carefully, Rocky searched the bank. He saw Gosi's hiding place of the night before. He found Gosi's trail to the look-out tree. He saw where Gosi had found the hickory nuts and made the repair to the cache. Rocky carefully helped himself to several pockets full of nuts, leaving the repair work to protect the rest.

Quickly he remounted Crown and raced back to the train, passing Gosi's hiding place without a glance.

Jeb heard Rocky's rapid approach and started back to meet him. So did Doc, panting and gasping. They all met with Bible John, sober and wishing otherwise.

"Hey, slow down, Brother," called Bible John, "We've a long way to go and no extra horses."

"Jeb, we've got us a trailer," reported Rocky. "Might be an Injun, but he's wearing crazy moccasins. His savvy ain't like no Injun."

"Do you think it's a young Indian proving himself?" asked Doc. He'd read about such things before he came west.

"Don't rightly know. If he is, he wants us to realize he's here. Never covered a single track. Must have been waiting for us to pass by this morning. Slept last night in a cave, ate berries from along the bank, even found a squirrel's cache. Oh, here, have some," said Rocky, offering the others a few of his hickory nuts. "It was this cache made me sure it wasn't no Injun. After he helped himself, he put sticks and stones over the hole to save the rest for the squirrels. Reckon no Injun ever done that."

"Did you say there's only one?" asked Jeb.

"Yep, just a half pint. His running stride was about half of mine, and when he walked it was even less. Seemed like one place he was dancing, steps were so twisted up. Besides, he ain't got much meat on him, either."

"Maybe it is a young Indian," said Doc again.

"Naw, no Injun, not even a real young one, would leave such tracks," answered Rocky.

"Unless it's a trick. Do you think it might be the kid?" asked Jeb. "You know the one I mean, the saddler kid?"

"Gol darn. You think so? Mebbe it is. If it is, though, he's gone now." Rocky looked doubtful.

"If he's eating berries and has scrounged some nuts, he'll be fit for today. Mebbe tonight he'll catch up with us," said Jeb thoughtfully.

"That's just fine and dandy, but when you catch him, who will take him back to his master?" asked Bible John. "We need everyone we have here to protect us."

"No sense worrying 'til we find out who it is," replied Jeb.

"What if your scout is wrong, and it is an Indian scout. What then?" asked Doc.

"That makes for a mite more trouble. If it's Injuns, means they're waiting 'til we cain't get help, and if we cain't stand them off, we lose," answered Jeb.

"What does that mean, we lose?" questioned Doc.

"Wal, that depends. We might only lose the train, we might lose just a couple of us, or we might all be taken prisoners. But, you can be sure if it's Comanches, we'll lose our scalps," explained Jeb.

"Even a hairless dome, like mine?" asked Doc, joking.

"Only needs a small tuft of hair to count coup, and you have enough," said Jeb. "Do you know how to handle that gun you have in you saddle bags?"

"I don't claim to be an expert, but I was given a gun and taught to shoot it before I got to Westport," replied Doc.

Tonight, unpack it and carry in on your person from now on. Mebbe you'll only need it for food. Mebbe it'll save your scalp," said Jeb. "Now, Bible John, are those bulges in your saddle bags whiskey bottles or guns?"

"I do have a gun, and I know how to use it. I also have a little medicinal whiskey," answered Bible John piously.

"Good. Tonight, unpack your gun and the whiskey. From now on you tote your gun, and I'll put the whiskey with our other medicine. You'll likely be needing both before you get to Cerrillos," ordered Jeb. "And now, one more word about our trailer. I want all of you to listen. The scouts and I will handle him. By morning we will know who it is and what he wants. Tonight, you both stay in camp with Cookie and stay quiet."

Rocky turned Crown back to continue his work of protecting the rear of the train, while Doc and the preacher returned to their places. Jeb hurried ahead to talk to Petre.

He found Flatnose riding with Petre. Jeb explained what Rocky had found and asked them to watch carefully for signs of others.

"There ain't nary a one ahead," said Flatnose. "Just returned from tonight's camp; ain't nary a sign. You can rest easy about that. If it is the kid, he'll stay hid for a couple more days, 'til we've gone far enough you won't be sending him back."

"Rocky says he's not covering his signs in any way, so probably he doesn't know enough to stay hid. We'll look for him after we've made camp," promised Jeb.

"No sense," said Flatnose. "That is, if we're sure it's the kid, wait 'til he's got the hungries real bad, and he'll march right into camp."

"You're probably right, but keep an extry eye out," said Jeb before he went back to explain to Cookie.

Gosi knew he had to be quiet. He made himself as flat as he could under the bushes and was glad the leather of his clothes was brown, almost the color of the earth. He was sure it helped hide him. He heard Rocky go by again; he was afraid the rider was going for help.

Gosi lay as if frozen to the spot until dark. He must have slept some, because he did not remember the gradual darkening as the sun went down—only one moment it was so bright he was afraid the rays would point him out, and the next moment it was the still darkness of night in the forest. What awakened him, probably was the horses and voices. Gosi listened.

Here's where he run off into the woods," Rocky said. "Figured I'd never catch him, so I went back over his signs."

You're right," said Jeb, "he'd be long gone as soon as he heard a sound. He's scared, and if you went chasing him, he'd run deeper and deeper into the forest and mebbe get real lost."

"Let's hightail it back to camp, and mebbe we'll catch him tomorrow," suggested Flatnose.

Not if I can help it, thought Gosi.

His heart sank. He knew now that Jeb was chasing him, and therefore he had no hope. Jeb never failed at anything. Gosi planned what he would do when Jeb caught him. One thing for sure—for the next few days he would be more careful and keep to his resolve of traveling only at night. Maybe, if he could get more than half way, they would take him on to Cerrillos.

Gosi thought of giving up, but what could he give up to? Life at Barnes Saddle Shop? Probably would not live through the ordeal. Nope, there was nothing to do but go on. So, on I go, decided Gosi.

Next morning the cook was up before dawn, frying bacon, making coffee, and baking fresh biscuits. He warmed the leftover beans, and breakfast was ready.

While Cookie was fixing the early meal, the two scouts had rounded up the mules and started to line them up for loading.

"Ain't mules something?" asked Petre. "It's a good kicking if you get them out of order."

"Worst time I ever had on a trip was when the Injuns stole the *mulera;* never expected to finish that journey," grunted Rocky as he placed a pack on the second mule.

"Wonder the dumb animals didn't leave you and find her," said Petre, as he made a mule squeal by pulling the cinch tight.

"Probably would've, but Jeb and me found the Injuns before they could butcher her, and we put a jack in her place," answered Rocky.

"Never heard of such a thing; did you have to fight?" asked Petre.

"Naw, we just traded the one for the other whilst they weren't looking," explained Rocky. "They were so busy, celebrating, they never saw anything. The chief had taken the bell off the *mulera's* neck and was jumping around the fire while he was ringing it, and the others were drinking the whiskey they had stolen. Jeb had another bell in his possible bag, so we skittered. Doubt those Injuns even noticed they were eating a jack and not a jenny."

"Did you wait to see?" teased Petre.

"No, siree! We took us one fast ride. As soon as the other mules heard the bell jingling, they all came running back into place, and we never stopped until we crossed Arkansas. That *mulera* was so glad not to be eaten she ran all the way." Rocky laughed as he remembered the scene.

"Hah, probably another of your big tales! But just the same, it's amazing to me that each mule knows its place and its pack. Why, once I saw a jenny almost kick a jack to death 'cause he tried to take her place in line. And that old jen was already loaded, too," said Petre.

"Cut out the jawing; come and get it!" howled Cookie.

About one hundred fifty yards away, hidden under a prickly thicket of wild blackberry bushes, Gosi's stomach growled and grumbled. He already had the hungries, he was exhausted and worse yet, he was scared. After the train left this spot they would start to cross an open prairie. Anyone could see for days. He wondered what he was going to do. He planned to run at night. Probably the train would knock down enough of the tall grass for him to follow them easily, but where was he to hide during the day?

In the camp, breakfast did not take long, and Cookie packed for the day. Each rider was given a packet of food for lunch, and as Jeb had instructed the night before, each was carrying his loaded gun.

"What's this?" asked Doc, as he received his packet of food from Cookie.

"It's your lunch," said Cookie.

"Does this mean we won't be stopping until night?" asked Doc.

"Yep," answered Petre. "If mules stop, they want to rest. When they rest, they want to lie down. If they lie down, they cain't get back up with their packs. So we'd have to unload and load each time. Better to eat in the saddle and keep moving."

Gosi's mouth watered. He would be glad to eat in the saddle if he had some of those biscuits. Maybe after they left, he could find something they had thrown away—if he could beat the little animals. He hoped that in their hurry, Cookie would not clean up very well. *Right now, even half a biscuit would be wonderful, a feast,* Gosi thought.

"Fall in! Fall in," shouted Jeb. "Come on, you goose-rumped goats, get your lazy carcasses in line and let's go. Move it, Cookie;

give old Bess a kick in the rump and get her bell jangling. We got twenty miles to make today. Consarn it, fall in, fall in, I say, or this morning may be your last. Hup! Hup and begone. Begone, I say. We got people standing line, waiting for us in Cerrillos. Get out and get going! Whooee, step it up , let's make that grass wave."

The mules loved this morning ritual; they would not start without it. Bess kicked a few side kicks, threw her head back and brayed. Next she began her trot, each step caused the bell to ring. The entire train responded and shuffled in step with the rhythm of the bell.

Flatnose was in the saddle before Cookie even began to make coffee. He traveled back far enough on the trail to be sure the person who was following the train was close by. He nodded to Cookie and Jeb so they could put the plan made the night before into action.

The team members had agreed that Cookie should 'accidently like' leave some food on a large leaf, atop one of the rock backing the campfire. Cookie even found one leaf with a deep dent, so it would hold beans easily.

Also, he was to leave a lunch pack; in case the person was not captured, he would still have food. Flatnose and Jeb hoped whoever it was would be hungry enough to try to find food at the campsite. They planned to circle back quietly and surprise him while he was eating.

This would be easy because Flatnose always roamed, and, Petre, the front scout, would ride in Jeb's place, so any Indians watching would not notice a great change. The men had discussed their hope that the trailer was the runaway from the saddlers, but they wanted to be prepared if an Indian was scouting their train.

Under Jeb's directions, the train fell into line and started through the sea of high, waving grass. As planned, the men on horses constantly changed position, riding first up and then back the length of the train so that eventually Jeb found a way to leave unnoticed.

Flatnose had circled only once before he left the train. After a short distance he dismounted and led his horse quietly around the back of last night's camp to a spot where he could watch and still not be seen. He waited there.

This time Gosi waited until the sun was about a quarter of the way up the eastern sky. The train had started westward just as the sun had appeared through a break in the trees. He wanted to crawl across to the camp right away, but he was a day wiser. He remembered the rear scout. He waited patiently until the sun was above the trees before quietly creeping out from under the prickly blackberry vines. His face and arms were scratched, and his hair stood in all directions—pulled by the thorns on the vines.

Good thing I've got leather clothes, thought Gosi, *otherwise they'd be ruined already*. Carefully, he tried to stand. He was so cramped, he was sure his legs were twisted sideways and his back must be going in at least two directions at once.

Keeping his thoughts and groans to himself, he walked the hundred and fifty yards toward the cold campfire. *I wouldn't mind if the squirrels have eaten a bit*, thought Gosi; *after all, I ate some of their cache, but so far I don't owe a bear one bite.*

By the time he reached the camp, most of his cramps and aches were gone. He joyously took the beans and bacon that Cookie had placed on the leaf. He started to gobble a big bite, but he was too hungry and his stomach's flip-flopping warned him that he must be careful. He took only a small bit of one of Cookie's biscuits and eyed the bacon and beans. As the biscuit hit his stomach, it relaxed, and Gosi could eat the rest of the feast.

Jeb and Flatnose watched. They waited until Gosi was eating the very last of the beans, pushed down by Cookie's biscuits, before they stepped from their hiding places.

"What are you doing here?" Jeb yelled his question.

Gosi dropped the leaf he was licking to get the very last of the bean juice. For the second time he started to run.

"Stop, you little beggar," yelled Jeb. "You'll get lost, and only the Injuns will find you. Now, listen to me. I know who you are, and if you want our help, you'd better buckle in and face us like a man."

Gosi looked back at the men and stumbled over a loose vine. He fell.

Flatnose picked him up. "Hold yer hosses, young 'un. Ain't nobody gone whip you here."

"Bring him in," yelled Jeb. He whirled Queenie around so he could hurry to tell the others and stop Doc and Bible John from worrying about facing Indians and losing their scalps.

Flatnose carried Gosi to his waiting horse, stooping to pick up the extra lunch packet on the way.

"Now, young 'un, if you ride quietly I won't tie you; any trouble from you, and I'll settle it."

"No trouble, no trouble," promised Gosi.

Flatnose rode on the blanket behind the saddle. Gosi sat in front on the saddle. His legs did not reach the stirrups, so he clung to the saddle horn and pinched his legs against the side of the horse to keep from slipping.

Holy Terror, Flatnose's horse, had no trouble carrying both of them the five miles forward to the train.

Thunder Birds of Legend *Rhea Coleman*

THREE

Because the wagon train could not stop and it was considered too dangerous for Gosi to slide from the saddle, it was necessary for Flatnose and Gosi to ride together all day. Flatnose continued to scout the area, first going forward to be with Petre and then ranging wide on each side before going back to be with Rocky. Through it all, Gosi kept his eyes open and his mouth shut.

Late in the afternoon, as they neared the site Jeb wanted to use for the night, Flatnose said, "Say, Kid, what's your handle?'

"My family call me Gosi."

"Gosi! Ain't no name for a scout. Your maw had it in for you for sure to name you that," said Flatnose disdainfully.

"Well, my whole name is Gustoferson," said Gosi.

"Gustoferson! Gol dang! A bear could finish you off 'afore anyone could call your name to warn you. Gustoferson! Won't do atall. Now, you take my advice and forget that name. Any kid that'd tackle a trip like this deserves a decent handle. From now on your name is Gutsy. Say, listen, I'll forget you ever told me the other name, and when we camp tonight, just say your name is Gutsy.—Naw just let me say your name is Gutsy."

"Right now, I'd agree to almost anything. If you think it'll help, that is," said Gosi—Gutsy.

"Darn tooting' it'll help. Man's got to have a real name to get by out here. Mine's Flatnose. Got it in a bawdy fight. Everyone knows Flatnose. If every you get in trouble, just say you're a friend of Flatnose, and at least fifty percent of the time you'll get help. Course, the other fifty percent, some 'un'll try to kill you," admitted Flatnose, almost proudly.

"Oh, Mister Flatnose. . . ," said Gutsy.

"Mister," spat Flatnose. "Ain't no misters out here either. Back East, where dandies live, I hear tell there are, but out here you get your respect by your actions. If you got guts, you get respect. If you ain't, you don't. Now what did you want?"

"What do you think they'll do to me when we get to the train?" asked Gutsy, trying to sound brave.

"Wal, first off, won't do nothing. Takes time to set up camp, unload the mules, and turn them out to graze," Flatnose said.

"I can help unload and take care of the animals. I know a lot about saddles," said Gutsy eagerly.

"Betcha do, Gutsy. Your best bet is to make yourself useful. Help Cookie and the scouts with the mules and whatever else. Them mules will be tired from carrying their load all day," replied Flatnose.

"Why don't we stop and rest them?" asked Gutsy.

"They'll work harder and longer than any other animal, but once they stop, they stop. So, it's better to just keep going," said Flatnose in his gravelly voice.

"Oh, then Cookie will fix a packet of food for noon each day," exclaimed Gutsy to show he understood.

"Yep, and you can eat it anytime, but once it's gone, it's gone. Hey now, hang onto the saddle horn, Gutsy. I see something ain't right over yonder," growled Flatnose as he heeled Holy Terror and reined him to the left.

"What can you see in all that tall grass?" asked Gutsy curiously.

"Wal, here's your first lesson in reading signs. See how the wind makes the grass wave back and forth?" asked Flatnose, pointing to the left.

"Pretty, isn't it?" answered Gutsy.

"See how it stops and then starts again a little later, making a line?" asked Flatnose.

"Like a pencil line," agreed Gutsy.

"Well, it could be a stream, it could be a break in the land, but more likely it's someone riding toward our train," said Flatnose.

"Who else would be out there?" asked Gutsy, the eager student.

"This time, it's probably some redskins, hoping to make a killing," answered Flatnose.

"Did you think it was an Indian that was following you before?" eagerly questioned Gutsy.

"Naw, you left too many greenhorn signs," said Flatnose, laughing.

"Signs! I just followed the train," said a surprised Gutsy.

"Yep, but didn't leave signs like a mule train. Not like an Injun neither. No Injun ever stopped to repair a nut cache for a squirrel," said Flatnose.

"You found that!" exclaimed Gutsy.

"No way to miss it. Now, shush, here's where I'll go ahead on foot. You stay on Holy Terror, and I'll look about a mite. But stay ready, we may want to leave here in one gosh almighty hurry," said Flatnose.

Gutsy watched. Flatnose moved silently and swiftly, making another stop-start in the waving, tall grass.

It seemed as if Flatnose was gone a long time; Holy Terror began to get as nervous as Gutsy, who felt lost and a good bit less than his name implied. He yowled in pure terror as Flatnose ran out of the tall grass, jumped up behind him, and kicked Holy Terror in the ribs at the same time.

"Lean down," commanded Flatnose, "and hang on! We're going to see who's fastest, old Holy Terror or that Injun pony that's coming on from behind."

"Indians! Are we going back to the train to help?" asked Gutsy.

"And lead that gol darned scout there? No, siree, we cut back to where Rocky should be, and he'll pick that redskin off our tail. Now hang on, I'm going to see if he's coming," whispered Flatnose.

"Flatnose, Flatnose, either we've found Rocky or there's more Indians ahead," whispered Gutsy, pointing to another line in the grass ahead.

"Grab that saddle horn tight; we're cutting loose. Keep your head down, let Holy Terror take his head! I'm gone take a potshot at our wild friend. When I do, Holy Terror will go like his name. Don't you get scared and fall off. Ain't got but two hands, myself, and they'll both be busy."

Flatnose hooked his feet in the stirrups, twisted sideways, and fired. Holy Terror ran as if he were possessed. Gutsy hung on to the saddle horn and squeezed hard with his bony knees. Flatnose held on to Gutsy and the reins. Someone in the direction of the racing Indian screamed.

"That'll cramp his style," crowed Flatnose as they tore through the long grass, Gutsy hanging on for dear life, trying to not get in Flatnose's way.

"Need some help?" yelled Rocky, coming at them from the opposite direction.

"Naw," answered Flatnose. "Saw an Injun and got a piece of him."

"Think he's dead?" asked Rocky, squinting in the direction of the disappearing line.

"Naw, ain't likely. It was a tricky shot; but it'll slow him, and we'll have time to get the train ready."

Rocky and Flatnose turned the horses in the direction of the train. Quite likely the others had heard the shots, surmised the problem, and would start preparing for the Indians, but just in case, they rushed to warn them and to help.

Jeb called, "Circle up, circle up."

Instantly Cookie started to circle the bell mule. By the time Rocky, Flatnose, and Gutsy had arrived, the circle was complete. Cookie had circled the mules once to get them into place and then a second time to close the space between the mules. He led the *mulera* to the center of the circle and stopped the train.

Patiently, the mules waited to be unloaded. Gutsy slid from Holy Terror and started to unbuckle and unload, even though the packs were about three-hundred pounds each.

"Hey, kid, you just unbuckle as fast as you can. Petre and me'll unload," shouted Rocky.

The packs were placed around the outside of the tight circle, each mule's pack in order. The animals lay down behind their packs, forming a small barricade.

Indians, as well as the mule skinner, knew mules became uncontrollable if they were frightened or excited, therefore, Jeb told Gutsy to ring the *mulera's* bell slowly to prevent the Indians frightening them into a stampede. As the animals relaxed, Gutsy realized the packs had become not only the barricade, but a small corral.

"Here they come," yelled Jeb. "Cookie, start coffee. Kid, keep that bell ringing slowly."

The band of Indians came whooping and yelling. Gutsy was so nervous he started to ring Old Bess's bell more rapidly, and the mules responded by standing.

"Slow down that gol darned bell," called Cookie.

Gutsy obeyed. The mules had started moving around inside the corral, as if practicing a slow march. Gutsy slowed the bell even more. The mules slowed, but continued walking inside the temporary corral until they reached their own pack. Then and only then did they settled down again.

"Injuns want whiskey," yelled the leader.

"No whiskey," answered Jeb. "How about some coffee and sugar?"

"Say, isn't that Bible Toting John?" the lead warrior asked in perfect English.

"Yes, my good man, how can I help you?" answered Bible John.

"Give my braves the whiskey you carry in your saddle bags. You can keep your Bible to help the white man," said the leader of the raiders.

"Charles? Is that you, Charles?" called a surprised Gutsy.

"Well, if it isn't my little white brother, Gustoferson! Did you finally get your nerve up to run away from Old Barnes?" asked the Indian.

"Three days ago, but why are you leading a band of Indians?" asked Gutsy.

"Now, little brother, Gosi . . . started the brave.

"His name is Gutsy!" shouted Flatnose.

"And your's is Flatnose," responded the brave. "I like your new name, Gutsy—it fits you. Mine is no longer Charles, now I am called Turning Red."

"But Chas—excuse me, Turning Red, does this mean you've left school?"

"It means I've decided to follow the heritage of my mother. You know I've never been white like my father, nor have I been Indian like my mother. So now I'm myself. I'm Turning Red."

"Well, Turning Red, our team welcomes you. Cookie is preparing us a feast; let's sit down, smoke a little, and talk 'til it's ready," said Jeb.

Cookie quickly rattled some pans and stirred the coffee in the pot, hoping the odor and the activity would convince the braves he was cooking food as directed.

"Don't care to talk to you, white man; you're as good as dead; but I'd like to talk with my friend, Gutsy. Maybe we can do a little trading. Gutsy, stop ringing that bell; my braves will not frighten your mules—at least not yet. There that's better, now we will talk. Jeb, have your men sit over there, behind you—except for the cook. He can prepare the feast. My braves will sit behind me except for Evening Star, he will guard your cook, in case he has any thoughts of being a hero."

"No such thoughts," stammered Cookie, "just want to cook the feast."

"Gutsy, we will do exactly as your friend asks. There's a pipe and tobaccy if you wish to smoke," said Jeb.

"He's too young to smoke. My braves will wait, also," responded Turning Red.

"It's good to see you, Turning Red. How long since you left school?" asked Gutsy, wondering how to continue.

"Remember the time you hid me in old Barnes's shed?" asked Turning Red.

"Sure do," said Gutsy. He grinned at his friend.

"Well, I went back to school. In the white man's school I learned about the laws of the Great White Father in Washington. I learned how my mother was considered a savage. At first I accepted everything, but when I returned to the trading post, I saw how my father was really the savage and my mother the civilized member of the family. I decided I would follow the ways of my mother. My father forced me to return to his civilization, but I lived with my mother's tribe each summer. This fall, I am not returning—I am Indian. Gutsy, why don't you join me? We'll teach you our ways, and you'd be my tribe brother."

"Thank you, Turning Red. I'd like to be your brother, but just like you, I'm born as I am. It's too late to change that now. What I must do is go to Cerrillos, work in the mines, and make lots of money so I can pay Old Barnes for my contract."

"Pay that old thief Barnes? But why, little brother? Let him rot, I say!" exclaimed Turning Red.

"No, no, Turning Red. When my paw bound me to Old Barnes to settle his gambling debt, he promised that if I didn't fulfill the contract, Herman would have to, and Herman is only nine," said Gutsy.

"Do you want us to settle that score for you?"

"No, Brother, I'd rather you'd help us all to get to Cerrillos so I can earn the money to buy the contract," replied Gutsy.

"Do you trust these people? Flatnose is well-known, and not all of it is good. Jeb is a good bullwhacker, but no more than that. Old Bible Toting John is famous for his love of whiskey," said Turning Red scornfully. "Want me to enumerate more of their ways?"

"But so far they have helped me, and I have no other way to get to Cerrillos," explained Gutsy.

"Then let's make a pact. As soon as it can be arranged, we will have a full tribal ceremony and everyone will know that you are my blood brother," offered Turning Red.

"Thank you, Turning Red," said Gutsy.

"As long as these men help you, we will protect them as well as you. This is our area, you will be safe here. Now, let's have that feast. We will celebrate both of our freedom—yours from Old Barnes and mine from the burden of the white man's way."

"What gifts can we give you in celebration?" asked Jeb.

"Whiskey from Bible Toting John's bag," replied Turning Red.

"I. . . I. . . d . . . don't have any," stuttered Bible John. "Jeb wouldn't let me have it."

"Maybe he's smarter than I thought," said Turning Red. "You know, Old Bible Toter, when you first came to my father's trading post, I thought you meant those things you said."

"Oh, I did, I did. I mean I do, I do," stammered Bible John.

"You do not! If you don't have the whiskey, it must be somewhere on the train. Probably labeled for medicinal purposes, eh, Bible John?" sneered Turning Red.

"Ah, medicinal, now there, perhaps I can be of service to you. I see one of the young men seems to have been shot. I have some ointment that might help," offered Doc.

"Yeah, like my dad's stuff he mixes up," taunted Turning Red.

"Possibly, but to ease his pain, just let him try mine," said Doc, offering him some salve.

He opened his saddle bag and gave Turning Red a jar of white ointment.

Grey Morning, nursing the wound he had received from Flatnose's bullet, put some of the soothing ointment on the wound. It did ease the pain. Grey Morning talked rapidly with Turning Red and the other braves, who joined in the conversation.

"He says it helps. Now the others want some," said Turning Red, translating.

"I have six jars; they may have them," said Doc

"There are nine braves," replied Turning Red.

"Perhaps three of them would like something else," said Doc.

"Are those surgical needles I see in your bag?" asked Turning Red.

"Yes, very fine surgical needles," answered Doc.

"Say, are you a real doctor?" inquired Turning Red. He eyed Doc up and down appraisingly.

"Yes," said Doc, as he watched some respect come into Turning Red's eyes.

"Give them each one of the needles," ordered Turning Red.

"What can I give the other three?" asked Doc.

"Is that green soap?" questioned Turning Red.

"Yes, antiseptic soap for injuries," replied Doc.

"Give the three others a bar of that soap," ordered Turning Red.

He explained each gift to the braves. He talked long about the magic properties of the soap if it were used on an open wound. The braves already believed the ointment was good. Carefully the braves examined the gifts. The potions were prized, but the most valuable to them was the strong steel needle with a hole in one end to put thread through the hole. They had only a bone punch with no hole in the end.

"You have not chosen a gift for yourself, Turning Red," invited Doc.

"Doc, I know that a real doctor has much knowledge that is needed by my people. Later I will claim my gift, with much interest added, by asking you to care for some of us. Now, I ask you to protect my brother who willingly took a whipping rather than tell my hiding place to Old Barnes," responded Turning Red.

"Oh, never mind that," said Gutsy. "If I hadn't been whipped for that it would have been for something else. Old Barnes believes in whippings."

"But you did it to protect me, and I am grateful," replied Turning Red.

"Come and get it! Come and get it!" called Cookie. "Ain't the greatest, ain't the worst. It's good fresh coffee, fresh biscuits, old beans, and new rice. Here, you'll like this dried buffalo; my friend, Jumping Over Cool Water, taught me how to make it. Come on, eat up, don't be shy!"

They came, and they ate every last biscuit, all the beans and rice, and every strip of the dried buffalo.

"You'll be safe across these plains," said Turning Red. "This is our territory. However, I know the Apaches are on the warpath; as usual some of your people offended them, and they plan to take revenge from those who travel on the Santa Fe Trail. I suggest you take the cutoff, the one you whites call the Cimarron Cutoff. It is desert, but it belongs to our people. You will be safer there."

"Thank you," said Jeb. "We are glad to know you and to have your promise of friendship."

"Save your breath, mule skinner. The only reason you are going on is because of my brother. The next train will not be so lucky. They will receive the treatment we planned for you. We'll use their trading goods and mules for our winter supplies."

"How about a mule to take back to your tribe?" offered Jeb.

"Looks like they are loaded pretty heavy," replied Turning Red.

"Maybe the women of your tribe would like some pots and pans, as well as the mule to carry 'em," said Jeb.

"How many pots do you have?" asked Turning Red.

"Twelve," said Jeb.

"How many pans?" asked Turning Red.

"For cooking, we are carrying ten," answered Jeb.

"What is done with the other pans?" asked the brave.

"Some are used to pan for gold," answered Jeb.

"Oh, yes, the white man's sickness," said Turning Red. "We'll accept a mule and ten of your pots, also eight of your cooking pans. We have a rope to lead the mule."

"Let me load it for you," offered Gutsy. "I learned about such things from Old Barnes."

"That one will load it," said Turning Red, pointing at Petre, "and he must hurry. We don't have much time, as my braves believe the evil spirits and the underworld come out during the dark, and we need to be back in our own camp while there is still some light."

"Do you believe that?" asked Gutsy.

"No, Gutsy, the white school taught me not to believe in my mother's gods, and the white men's actions taught me not to believe in theirs."

"What do you believe in ?" questioned Gutsy.

"Nothing. It's easier that way," replied Turning Red.

"Will we meet again soon?" asked Gutsy.

"You can be sure of that. If you find your choice to stay with these white men wrong, my tribe will welcome you. I'll train you to be my helper."

"Thank you, Brother. I would like to come for a visit. When I have a home, you will be the most welcome of all my guests."

Turning Red nodded, whirled his horse, and started toward his distant wickiup, leading the loaded mule behind him.

His braves followed, heads high, backs straight, and eyes constantly moving from side to side, watching for any disturbance that might mean danger for them.

FOUR

Even before the first inquiring fingers of the sun appeared over the eastern horizon, Cookie was making coffee, Flatnose was scouting the area, while Jeb and the scouts were preparing the pads and packs for the mules.

Gutsy tried to spring up from his saddle blanket bed, spread on the grassy ground, but his spring was more like the determined efforts of an old man.

Doc grinned knowingly at Gutsy and said, "I'm not sure which is worse, lying on the hard ground with a saddle for my pillow or riding in that same saddle all day long."

"Hey, Gutsy, even heroes have to work on this train," shouted Cookie. "Bring that slab of fat back and stir the beans, while I cut a slice of meat for everyone."

"And when you're done, get another lead rope out of my possible sack, so you can learn how to lead a team of mules," added Jeb. "We got thirty miles to cover today, so let's get cracking."

"Hey, watch those biscuits, kid. You'll hate burned bread sure enough if you have it for lunch," shouted Petre.

"Stir those beans one more time and then start laying those saddle blankets on the backs of those misbegotten beasts. Make sure you get them on the right ones. Mules are plumb fussy about such things," shouted Rocky.

"How'll I know if it's the right one?" asked Gutsy.

"If you don't get kicked, it's the right one; if you do, try another. Step to it now, ain't no time to hesitate. When you're done, it'll be time to eat.

Gutsy hurried to comply, anxious to please.

"Come and get it, come and get it," called Cookie. "Ain't got time for niceties, just load up and dig in."

"Hey, look out, Flatnose. You'll get us all dusty," said Rocky as Flatnose pulled Holy Terror to a rump-down stop at the edge of the camp.

"Good thing. Don't hold food for no one. Come and get it! Consarn it, Flatnose, I've got other things to do than wait for you," grumbled Cookie.

"Gutsy's friends are close, but their bellies are filled, and they're sleeping. For me, I'm blamed grateful for that whipping you took, Gutsy," said Flatnose. But I'm still a little uneasy."

"We got no other choice but to go on," said Jeb.

"Say, Cookie, you know this coffee is just the best ever! Biling hot, black as a bear, with the kick of a mule! Ain't for the weak, but for us men of the trail—it's the way it ought to be," said Flatnose.

Doc struggled to swallow his.

Bible John watched and then whispered, "It'd go down easier if we had a little medicinal whiskey in it."

"Say, Gutsy, you gonna' try some of this joe?" asked Rocky.

"Every man of the trail needs coffee," urged Petre, hoping for a little fun.

"Here, kid, this is yours," said Cookie, handing a cup to him that had a little more water than coffee in it.

"Not bad," lied Gutsy, "ought to keep me going all day."

He took a deep breath, finished the cupful, and before he could be offered another, he ran back to help load the mules.

The packs were spread out in a line and each mule had claimed its own. Petre and Rocky loaded, while Gutsy placed a piece of matting over the load and secured it with ropes and cinches. The trick was to pull the cinches so tight the mules would squeal.

This made for a more comfortable day for the animal. Here was where expertise was needed. If the load was too loose, it would slip; it might even slip under the belly of the mule, causing, at best, a delay. Often it would injure the animal. Part of the scout's job, which now became part of Gutsy's job, was to constantly check the way the loads were riding. He was to walk up and down the line checking for any problems.

Each day the entire loading and unloading process would be reenacted. Each mule would be loaded and cinched. Then Petre must yell, *"Adios!"* (good-bye). Rocky must respond, *"Vaya!"* (go). Next, Petre must shout, *"Anda!"* (move). Then, and only then, the mules would move forward to their places in line.

It took about five minutes to load each mule. If only the two scouts were working, more than two and a half hours was needed to ready the team. However, Cookie and Jeb formed a second team, while Flatnose and Gutsy helped wherever they were needed. So the thirty-nine mules were ready to travel in a little over an hour.

Cookie finished packing the lunches and passed them to the travelers before he took his place astride the bell mule *(mulera)*.

Doc put his aching body back into the saddle. He sighed. Even after four days, he still had saddle burn and felt as if he had been shaken together and tamped down. He'd never make a trainmaster.

Bible John was beginning to feel the rhythm of the ride. Four days without whiskey was a long time, but he did admit to feeling better.

Flatnose, ever ready to start roaming, watched the caravan start with anticipation. The scouts urged the last mule into place and mounted their horses, ready for the day's duties.

Jeb yelled, "Fall in! Fall in! Come on, you goose-rumped goats. Get your lazy carcasses in line and let's go. Move it, Cookie. Step lively there, Gutsy, show us what an eager kid can do. Come on, old Bess! We got thirty miles to do today, and if you want to see tomorrow's sunrise, you'd better move it on out. Hup, hup, and begone. Begone, I say. Cain't you see those folks lined up, waiting for us in Cerrillos? Now, Cookie, give old Bess her kick and let's go. Whooee! Step it up, step it up, I say. Let's make that sea of grass look like a tidal wave struck it. Giddap! Giddap!"

Gutsy stepped out quickly on this, his first full day with the team. He pulled on his rope, and the *mulera* started, the bell began to ring. Quickly, each of the mules moved forward to follow the bell ringer.

Jeb watched the sun finish its climb over the horizon, sending brilliant rays forward over the grass.

"Ain't that a sight?" asked Rocky as he halted his horse next to Jeb.

Together they enjoyed the beauty of the morning rays playing on the tall grasses, spreading their colors of sepia and silver ahead as far as a person could see. The grasses waved and rolled in the morning breeze, shimmering and glistening.

"Cain't believe it can be even more beautiful at sunset, cain you? Just you wait; Doc will be writing more in his book, and

Gutsy will be learning colors he ain't seen afore. I say this is God's country," exclaimed Flatnose. "Hope when my times comes to check in, it'll be in this part of the country and my spot will be where the sun rises and sets on the shimmering prairie grass."

"Didn't know you were a poet, Flatnose," said Rocky, teasing.

"Don't need to be a poet to know beauty when you see it. Just 'cause I cain't write, don't mean I cain't see and feel." Flatnose wheeled Holy Terror and moved out.

"Folks can sure be surprising," said Rocky. "To look at his buckskin trousers and hunting shirt, you'd never think he was anything but the half-wild trapper he's supposed to be."

"Trappers are strange men. They live alone most of the time, eat only the meat they catch. They never seem to need companionship, but when they do choose a companion they are utterly loyal and helpful," said Bible John.

They'll share their last bit of food with a stranger, but Gawd Almighty, if they hate you, and they hate easy, they will track you down and finish you," said Petre. "Why they even smile as they are doing the person in."

"Well now, we know that at least one trader is part poet," said Jeb, as each man moved to do his own work.

Hours passed, with only the sounds of the ringing bell, the braying mules, talking to each other, and the noise of the shuffling trot as they followed the old trail made by herds of buffaloes over the centuries.

The sun was beginning to lower in the western sky when Jeb called: "Circle up, circle up. We've made our thirty miles for today. We'll set up camp here."

"Whooee, if we've made thirty miles," said Gutsy, "I must have walked and run at least forty."

His job required him to walk the entire length of the train on the left side and back up it on the right, every hour, checking the ropes that cinched the loads to the backs of the mules. He almost split with pride because none of the animals had needed to be reloaded. Success felt good, but he was tired. Making saddles did not work the same muscles as leading a team did.

"Do you wish you were back at your bench in Westport?" asked Petre as he watched Gutsy rub his legs.

"For a fact, no," answered Gutsy. "My legs may be tired, but if I was back in Westport my back would be bloody raw and aching.

Right here is exactly where I want to be."

"That's good, 'cause now we unload these beasts," said Rocky.

"Do you want me to take the loads off after I uncinch them?" asked Gutsy, remembering the night before when he was told to only uncinch.

"Nope, you uncinch them first, and then go gather more fuel for the fire so Cookie can get the coffee biling." Jeb decided this after a pause.

"Here, Doc," called Jeb, "see if you can spread the packs out to air. Bible John, take the horses and give them some water and feed before you hobble them. It'll help you pass the time until Cookie gets the coffee ready."

Gutsy uncinched the ropes holding the packs, found a load of buffalo chips, which he added to the fire that Cookie had started with dry grass.

By this time, the scouts had unloaded almost half the mules. The mules brayed and pranced, stretching their legs and voices, as their burdens were removed. There was no silence on the prairie now.

Gutsy was excited as he returned to camp. But with the mule's music he could hardly be heard as he yelled, "Cookie, Cookie, I've made a discovery. You've already told me we are traveling over a known trail, even said it had been used for years, but I'm sure of something else. You see, Cookie, I went ahead to get this load of buffalo chips and try my hand at reading some signs. The grass is still bent forward, as you said, but when I started to pick up the chips some were very dry, some were middling dry and some weren't dry at all."

Cookie nodded.

"Since the grass was bent ahead, and the chips were fresh, I fingered there's been a herd through here just a while ago," continued Gutsy.

"Why'd you suppose they'd go that way?" prodded Cookie.

"I don't know. Maybe they have a summer home somewhere ahead of us, or maybe they are going to a watering hole," said Gutsy.

"You could be right on both ideas, but since buffaloes usually are on the move, I'd put my money on the fact that they know the Arkansas is just ahead of us," said Cookie as he piled more chips under the already boiling coffee.

"I hope I see a herd of buffalo. Do you think I will?" asked Gutsy.

"If you mean before you die, Lawdy, yes! Probably you'll see them by the thousands. If you had a horse, you'd probably be able to go with Jeb today, and might even get us one for food, but as it is, we'll travel with the team and keep it moving," answered Cookie.

"Will we catch up with them, do you know?" asked an excited Gutsy.

"Mebbe not that herd, but probably lots of them are gathering at the Arkansas. It's spring, you know, so probably there will be other herds coming to meet these," explained Cookie. "I don't want to get into the subject of young buffalo and rutting and babies at this time. Takes too long to settle all those points."

"What are you stuffing into his head now?" asked Jeb.

"He's found fresh buffalo droppings, and I was saying we might be eating fresh meat for supper tomorrow," answered a grinning Cookie.

"Is that right, Gutsy?" queried Jeb.

"Yes, sir," said Gutsy.

"Now wait. Let's get something straight right now. No yes sirs. This is a team working together. I'm the boss, but I'm not wanting to be called sir. I figger a man's a man as long as he acts like one; so far you've acted like one, so the name's Jeb."

"All right. When I was gathering chips for the fires, some were very dry, some were new piles. That's what I told Cookie, and he said probably the herds are gathering for spring duties," answered Gutsy.

"Probably right. I'll have the scout look for them tomorrow. Well, look at that. Here comes Flatnose, pushing his hoss as if he has news. We'll wait for him to tell us what it is before we say you've found something," said Jeb.

Flatnose dismounted hurriedly.

"Howdy, Flatnose. Pretty dull day, wasn't it?" called Jeb.

"Today mebbe dull, but tomorrow we can have us a passel of fun chasing buffalo. Big herd grazing about ten miles over east, heading for the Arkansas. We could surprise them in the morning and fill our food baskets," answered Flatnose, eyes sparkling. "I was thinking of the chase."

"Sounds good to me. Let's finish getting the camp ready for the night and do our planning," said Jeb.

This night the mules were staked because of their nervousness at the nearness of the wild bison. The packs were readied for quick loading. Cookie made extra batter for the morning hot bread.

Gutsy went after several more loads of buffalo chips; the fire would be kept going all night, not only to cook the morning beans, but to keep any wild animals, fleeing from the buffalo, away from the camp. He was careful to stack the chips far enough away so they would not burn accidentally, yet close enough to be easy to add to the fire during the night.

"Come and get it, come and get it," called Cookie.

Everyone quickly gathered for huge cups of boiling black coffee, beans, fresh biscuits, and a little dried buffalo meat.

"Let's make plans for tomorrow after we've sampled Cookie's offerings," said Jeb.

After the silent first round was finished and plates refilled, everyone was ready to begin their planning session.

Jeb said, "Come on, lad, sit here and listen. Mebbe you'll learn something useful. Flatnose, Rocky, Petre, and you have all found fresh signs of buffalo. It's about time. Cookie tells me we can use some fresh meat. Also, we must prepare for the next leg of our trip. We are almost to the Arkansas; once't we get across that river, we travel over desert. It'll be good to stay over a couple of days to give the animals a rest, and let them fill up on water. We can use those hours to jerk some meat so we can carry it without spoilage in the hot, dry desert climate.

"If we have reasonable luck we will have a hide or two to clean. The thickest one will be for you, Gutsy, so your bed will be a little softer," explained Jeb. "The other hides are for some fine new moccasins to wear as we ride into Cerrillos with our load."

Everyone nodded in agreement.

"In the morning we will load the team as usual and start out. Those who have hosses will take a little detour and bring down a few buffalo. The closer to the Arkansas, the better, so we won't have to carry them so far.

"Cookie and Gutsy will be responsible for the train. I know you can do it—I've watched you both work today. This will only take a few hours, and we'll all enjoy our feed of fresh buffalo steaks tomorrow night," continued Jeb. "Flatnose, you've had much experience with this type of work; tell the others what is the best way."

"Been on a hunt or two myself," grumbled Bible John.

"Mebbe true, and some evening around the campfire you can tell us about them, but right now Flatnose is going to tell you just how we want it done this time," replied Jeb.

Flatnose explained many points of hunting buffalo, including the fact that they will not notice a gunshot if they have not seen a hunter or smelled his scent. He had a plan where they could get the few that were needed and not disturb the herd. He suggested they stay upwind, out of sight, just killing the ones needed to finish the trip as far as Fort Union.

Doc listened carefully before he said, "Say, do you think I might be more help with the team. Seems to me that two people will be kept pretty busy, and I might help by riding up and down, checking the loads."

"What's the matter, Doc, are you a little yellow in the spine?" asked Rocky.

"I may be, I'm not sure. I've learned a lot of new things traveling with you, and I feel I can help with the mules. I am not prepared to be a buffalo hunter, though," countered Doc.

"You may be right; you see, we don't want a big kill. We don't have animals to carry extra meat and hides, even if we could prepare them for the desert. If you want to wait until another time for your buffalo, it's fine with me," said Jeb.

"How many do you think?" asked Flatnose.

"Oh, thousands," said Petre. "The herd is huge."

"I mean, how many can we really use?" asked Flatnose.

"Even if we use only the humps, the hearts, the tongue, and the skins, we cain't use more than three."

"See! We can easily bring that back without Doc's horse, and he's right, it'd be better to have a horse here. Thank you, Doc, for volunteering," said Flatnose.

"Volunteering. Ha! He's scared, that's what he is," muttered Petre.

"Speaking of being scared," said Flatnose, "if a man ain't, I don't want that fool with me. Why, he might shoot hisself, or, worse yet, me. Only a dunce ain't got sense enough to be scared when a herd of crazy buffalo faces him."

"If we are just going to kill two or three, probably won't even make them stampede," said Rocky.

"That's best. Never can depend on what those dumb critters will do in a stampede. If you think mules are dumb, let me tell you they are real smart compared to a herd of buffalo who has a mad on," said Flatnose.

"Morning comes quickly, especially when there's buffalo to be gotten, so let's hit the sack. Flatnose, take the first watch; Petre, the second; and Rocky the last one. I'll be checking on each one of you. Don't let me catch you asleep," ordered Jeb.

"Rocky, if you'll stir me a little about halfway through your watch, I'll put the biscuits on and make fresh coffee," offered Cookie.

"When can I take a turn at the watch," asked Gutsy.

"When you have a hoss and a gun. For now, be prepared to get up and help with breakfast and mules. Mebbe you'll own a buffalo skin to sleep on in a few days, but I cain't figger any way to get you a hoss before we get to San Miguel," replied Jeb.

Gutsy made his bed with the mule's saddle pads. He watched longingly as the others used their saddles for pillows and placed their guns within easy reach. He saw they only loosened the knives kept strapped to their boots.

First, Flatnose prepared his bed, fortified himself with a fourth huge trail cup of coffee and the last biscuit from supper. He began his watch by walking up and down the trail. Satisfied that all was well, he found the highest spot possible in the flat prairie, tethered his saddle horse, and settled down with his rifle primed at his side.

FIVE

"Let's get this morning started," whispered Cookie as he shook Gutsy awake. "It'll be a long one, and we'll need every minute of it."

Gutsy stood up, shook the blades of grass out of his hair, twisted his leather britches and shirt to a little more comfortable position on his skinny body, and looked up at the sky, lit only by the morning star.

"What's first?" Gutsy whispered as he pulled on his moccasins.

Cookie had already started coffee with the water Gutsy had brought from the spring the evening before. The beans had cooked all night by the fire. The batter bread Cookie had prepared the night before was already baking in the dutch oven.

Only the meat needed to be cut and fried, so Cookie said, "Get the hosses and the mules from their grazing spot and start to lay on the saddle blankets. Watch 'em closely, 'cause they're antsy on account of the buffalo. Best bring in the hosses first."

Gutsy located the hobbled horses and returned them to camp. The scouts, awakened by the smell of coffee boiling and bread baking, joined him.

They went after the mules, but not before Jeb cautioned: "All animals sense moods quickly, mules especially, and they are uncontrollable when you get them overexcited."

"Hey, Gutsy, pull the *mulera's* stake first," called Rocky. "Like Jeb says, we have to keep the mules happy."

"It's going to take a while to get all of them thirty-nine stakes out of this hardpan," grumbled Petre.

"Start near old Bess," suggested Gutsy. "I poured a bucket of water on each stake, so it'd pull out easier, and I started over there."

"Say, for a green-stick lad, you've got a lot of ideas," complimented Rocky. "How'd you ever get on to this one?"

"Remember, I'm from the clay country of Missouri," grunted Gutsy as he pulled another stake. "I've seen my paw do this."

"Good for your paw. Hope he taught you lots of these kinds of tricks," said Rocky as he slapped another mule on the rump to make it follow old Bess to the loading area.

The stakes were pulled, and they were coiling the ropes so they could be used to cinch the loads, when they heard the favorite call of the day.

"Come and get it, come and get it! Ain't got time for niceties, so come along and dig in."

Eagerly, they all obeyed.

"Buffaloes are grazing this direction—should be in easy carrying distance of tonight's camp, just about noon," reported Flatnose. "Got company. Gutsy's friends. May upset our apple cart a mite."

"Char. . . I mean, Turning Red?" asked Gutsy in surprise.

"Yeah, Turning Red and about a hundred of his kinfolk," snorted Flatnose.

"A hundred!" repeated Gutsy.

"Yeah, no doubt getting their year's supplies," answered Flatnose.

"A hundred!" repeated Gutsy.

"Yeah, I hope it really is only their supplies they are after," answered Flatnose.

"But he won't let them hurt us, remember, he promised," reminded Gutsy.

"Well, Gutsy, this may be the time you learn a promise ain't always what you think it is," said Flatnose.

"Oh, don't worry. I know Turning Red. His promise will be a good promise," assured Gutsy.

"Hope you're right," said Jeb. "Say, mebbe we can have a little fun and help Gutsy's friends get their supplies."

"We plan to camp tonight for the last time on United States soil. Even thought we might stay for a day or so, resting the team, preparing the buffalo meat and the hides. Now, we'll wait and see how things work. However, nothing's changed until we're forced to change it. Let's get the train ready and on its way, just as if we didn't know about the Comanches," said Jeb thoughtfully.

Everyone helped. Doc gathered the packs together; Bible John joined Cook to load the mules; first the cooking equipment, then the packs of merchandise. Petre and Rocky worked together, racing Flatnose and Jeb, loading the packs Doc had gathered. Gutsy wrapped the ropes around the loads and tightened them. Each mule screamed as the cinch was tightened.

Petre and Rocky alternated with Jeb and Flatnose going through the ritual of one loader calling *"Adios,"* the second responded correctly with *"Vaya,"* and the first shouting *"Anda!"*. Surprisingly, those dumb animals knew which pair of men's instructions they were to respond to, and just when they should move to find their proper place in line.

Less than two hours after Gutsy's first glimpse of the morning star, he was leading the thirty-nine loaded mules down the old buffalo trail, heading for his dream of freedom and wealth, whistling a tune and thinking about his good fortune.

As planned, Jeb, Bible John, Rocky, and Petre were not with the train, but off to the northwest, preparing to meet the buffalo herd before it crossed the Arkansas banks.

"Don't you wish you could see the buffalo herd?" asked Gutsy.

"Seen enough, now I like them best dead! But, if you keep this train going, mebbe you'll see some of them," said Cookie. "Say, Doc, why don't you give Gutsy a ride and we'll make this team hurry a little."

"That's a fine idea. First I'll ride up and down the line, checking the loads, while Gutsy gets ready to ride with me," agreed Doc.

After Gutsy mounted Doc's horse, Cookie kicked old Bess and cracked his whip in the air. Startled, old Bess began to trot. This caused her bell to ring faster and faster. The mules of the train hurried to keep up with the rhythm.

"Say, Jeb, I'm glad we don't have old Doc to watch out for," said Petre. "In my opinion, he'll never make a buffalo hunter."

"Probably not, but he's a better trail rider than he was the first day," answered Jeb.

"Yeah, whatever is the matter with him, it isn't his stomach, he can eat as much as I can. Don't turn his nose up at nothing."

"Lost a lot of blubber, too," said Flatnose. "Noticed him cinching in those fancy britches of his'n. Figure purty soon there'll be enough extry to make Gutsy a pair."

"Yep, and he'll be needing them," agreed Bible John.

"Wal, if we get him a bed today and mebbe enough tough leather to make us all moccasins, that'll be a start," said Jeb.

"*Yeeii*, Jeb! Lookee over there. Injuns coming to visit. Hope they still plan to hunt buffalo and not us!" shouted Rocky.

"Men, be calm—whatever it is we'll handle it. First of all we talk. Injuns always talk. No need to worry until we finish conflabing, so smarten up and be friendly like," said Jeb.

"Hello, Turning Red," greeted Jeb.

"Hello, mule skinner. Where's Gutsy?" responded the brave.

"Ain't got a horse nor a gun, so he's leading the mule train while we try to get a bit of fresh meat for the trip along the cutoff. You doing the same?" asked Jeb.

"Right, we need fresh meat now and supplies for winter. The herd, as you know is heading for water at the Arkansas. If you stay on the eastern side of the herd and we work the western side, we could slaughter enough for all," said Turning Red.

"You're right. We need two or three. More than that would spoil. We could use several skins, one to make a bed for Gutsy and two others for moccasins. However, with our guns, we could kill many. The rest could be for your tribe," offered Jeb.

Head erect, back straight, with eyes blazing, Turning Red answered, "My braves have bows and arrows. We will take our share of buffalo. However if you are going to waste the animals our tribe is very large, and we will accept what you don't need. We will camp beside the Arkansas where the women will prepare the meat for the winter."

"Good. Then you will see Gutsy, because we plan to camp there also."

"You must be our guests at a feast," said Turning Red. "Our women will prepare it. We will celebrate the great buffalo kill of today, and Gutsy and I can have the tribal ceremony that will prove to all that we are blood brothers. You white men will carry that story with you to Cerrillos," commanded Turning Red.

We consider it an honor to be invited to both celebrations," answered Jeb.

"First let's take care of providing the women with lots of meat for the feast, Remember, you are on the left, we are on the right. We will have a contest to see who are the greatest hunters," shouted Turning Red as he rode off.

"A contest!" snorted Flatnose. "Guess it's about right, though; five men with guns and fifty to sixty braves with bows and arrows—and one gun—Turning Red's."

The hunters rode on quietly for about an hour before Rocky whispered, "Here comes our herd."

"This isn't the largest herd I've seen," said Bible John, "but still, it's impressive."

As the buffaloes become larger and larger blots, the hunters decided on their strategy. They would separate; the herd was calm and, as yet, had taken no notice of them. If they continued to be unobserved, they could choose only young calves and cows and not cause a stampede.

The blots continued to grow larger; the hunters carefully stayed upwind and out of sight. Soon the animals were so close they could distinguish individual beasts. Rocky and Petre decided it was time to leave the group. Next Bible John and Flatnose rode away.

Before they left Jeb said, "Pick a nice calf or two for us, then have fun. These Comanches need food. When they count how many our guns have killed, compared to their bows and arrows, I want glory written all over us. The more the merrier, then, perhaps, they will have respect for our guns at least."

Jeb rode to his place at the back of the herd.

Each hunter had his pet theory on how best to kill a buffalo. Because the hide is tough, especially over the hump, Petre believed his best shots should go between the red eyes. Rocky felt it was easier to put the bullet so it angled to the brain through the nose and mouth, while Flatnose preferred to shoot the beast in the heart.

Since only a quarter of the animal's height was below the breast bone, an off-angle front shot, lower than most, was needed. Flatnose knew he was an expert at this shot. However, this time all three methods were equally successful. Three shots were fired, three animals lay dead, apparently unnoticed by the rest of the herd. The hunters, also, rode on, still upwind and off to the side, which prevented the herd from either seeing or smelling them.

Within seconds Jeb and Bible John also had their animals. A surprised young bull looked up, walked a few steps, his hind legs folded, and he died. A cow also tumbled and died as it rushed toward the men.

On the other side of the large herd, the braves, afraid of not winning the contest, started whooping and shouting. Instantly the buffaloes began to stampede toward the white hunters.

Recognizing the danger, the five men drew together, firing as they moved. The shots were true; they downed buffalo almost every time. Not only did the men want to kill buffaloes, but they hoped to scare the animals into running in another direction. However the buffaloes were enraged enough to rush the men, who continued shooting from the close group. The dead beasts began to pile one on the other. Still, nothing stopped the animals. They ran blindly forward, building up a barricade around the men.

Excitement caused the horses to snort and buck. The hunters tried to shout louder than the roar of the stampede. Jeb fired directly into the flaming red eyes of the new lead buffalo. It fell atop the last leader, The mound of dead animals grew higher. The men drew their horses closer behind the pile, now a four foot barricade. True to the reported stupidity of the bison, the herd rushed forward, and more were killed.

Suddenly Flatnose left the relative safety of the group. He galloped along the side of the herd, shouting and shooting, trying desperately to turn the herd. He feared that the herd would continue to run wild in the wrong direction and join up with the mule train. If this happened the mules would be carried with it in its crazy race.

As the herd reached the men and the pile of dead animals, it swerved suddenly, with the gracefulness of a planned ballet. The hunters, horses, and dead buffalo were neither bruised nor touched. Looking from a distance it seemed a planned maneuver.

Flatnose quickly rejoined the hunters. They shot, reloaded, fired, reloaded, fired, reloaded, and fired until the crazed herd turned away from the mule team and outdistanced the hunters.

Team members returned to the area where the buffalo lay slaughtered. They joined Turning Red and his braves who were counting. Travois and other equipment were on the field, brought by the women, whose day's work had just begun. Jeb selected three young animals; he started to skin and clean one.

Turning Red appeared immediately. "You have killed seventy-two buffalo. We have killed twenty. You and your guns are the victors. Our women will prepare your animals," announced Turning Red, indignantly.

"But your squaws have much work. We can do three. The rest are for you and your tribe," argued Jeb.

"Our women will clean the ones you have selected. They will be ready for you at camp tonight. Also, Swiftly Running Feet will prepare three hides. I understand one is to be for the bed of my brother, therefore, we will choose the thickest for him.

"Tonight we will feast, but for now take this hump with you; a tender buffalo steak, fixed by your own cook, will only whet your appetites for the food our women will prepare. My scouts tell me your team is almost to the Arkansas, so you must hurry on your way and help them hold back the mules from the water," said Turning Red.

He presented Jeb with a huge bloody hump of a buffalo.

"Flatnose, I understand you like tongue best, so here, carry this to your cook. It is a special gift to you from Flower With A Yellow Face," Turning Red said gravely as he presented a fresh buffalo tongue to Flatnose.

"We thank you for this. I am sure your squaws are better at preparing the meat than we are," Jeb lied.

"Then be on your way and tell the news to my brother that tonight we will have our ceremony."

Turning Red turned away from the nervous white men and began to give directions to the women as to which of the buffaloes were to be prepared for the mule skinner and his men.

"Do you believe him?" questioned Rocky, as they rode away.

"Cain't tell," replied Jeb.

"Wal, I say we better believe him," said Flatnose. "You know the reason he let us go on was because we have Gutsy with us. Thank Gawd we still have Gutsy."

I'd say we are uncommonly lucky to have him with us," agreed Bible John. "Terrible he had to take a whipping for anyone, but I'm grateful he did."

"You know, I've always heard that if an Injun is hurt by a person, that Injun's tribe never rests until someone of the other man's tribe is injured worse. Mebbe it works in reverse. I mean, mebbe a good turn must be returned," suggested Flatnose.

"Seems to be that way with Turning Red, anyway," agreed Rocky. "Do you know who his pap be?"

"Yeah, we all know," said Flatnose. "He owns a big fort out among the Ioways. He married Turning Red's mother, sister of the Ioway chief, so he could be protected; but he's never been a faithful nor kind husband. Guess now his son will make him pay.

SIX

"Whooee-yiee," called Rocky, as the hunters reached the train.

"Cookie, slow that team or we'll have a stampede of loaded mules," ordered Jeb, riding quickly toward old Bess. Pulling even harder on the reins, Cookie panted and finally managed to say, "Won't work—they smell the water—there's no stopping them."

Reining his horse to the front of the team, Petre tried to pace them.

He called, "Doc, you and Gutsy join me. Old Bess is used to Gutsy. It's still a mile to the water—we gotta stop them, or they'll run into the river, packs and all."

Flatnose rode up the left side of the team. He uncurled his rope, whirled it over his head several times, and placed the loop exactly over old Bess's head. He pulled the rope to slow her down. Cookie leaned forward, muffled the bell quickly, then he rang it very very slowly. The mules began to slow.

"Circle up! Circle up," called Jeb, as he realized the team was again under control.

Doc and Gutsy led the team in a circle. Cookie and Flatnose pulled and yanked until the entire team formed a reasonable-looking circle. Everyone but Cookie hurried to unload the animals, so they could go to the river. Cookie stayed with the *mulera*, slowly ringing her bell. When the last mule was uncinched, its pack on the ground, Cookie dismounted.

Quickly, yet carefully Gutsy removed the saddle and the cooking pans from old Bess. Cookie gave her a slap on her rump, yelled, "*Vaya!*" and stepped back. Thirty-nine mules, freed from their packs, thundered down the steep sand banks of the Arkansas River to roll and cavort like children playing in the water.

"Thank the Lawd you got here," gasped Cookie. "Those animals smelled what they wanted, and I couldn't hold them."

"They're extra nervous from the smell of the buffalo herd and the noise from the shots," soothed Jeb.

"Boy, you sure did a lot of shooting," exclaimed Gutsy.

"Didn't you get any?" asked Doc looking around, mystified.

"First news first," said a smiling Jeb. "We are attending a feast tonight, prepared by the squaws of Turning Red's tribe. They are cleaning our buffalo for us. However, we do have a tongue and a hump for right now. Reckon everyone could stand a little fresh buffalo."

"I could sure go for a cup of Cookie's coffee," said Flatnose.

"We could celebrate with a little medicinal whiskey," timidly suggested Bible John.

"No whiskey, and don't mention that word while we are with the Comanches," ordered Jeb sharply.

"Help fix camp—we'll start some coffee," said Cookie, "but if we do, all story telling must wait."

"Even about Flower with a Yellow Face?" teased Rocky.

"Especially about Flower With Any Kind of Face," responded Cookie.

"Gutsy, you'll have to go upstream for clean water. The mules have muddied it here. There's plenty of wood, so these frisky ones can get the fire started," said Jeb.

"Flower With A Yellow Face," said Cookie. "Ha!"

"Don't fuss, Cookie, she gave a buffalo tongue to Flatnose, so she must be kindhearted," said Rocky, laughing.

"Kindhearted," said Cookie, snorting. "You'd better be mighty careful, Flatnose. Never knowed an Injun to give anything without wanting something in return."

"Well, betcha she'd be busy making me coffee after a big hunt like this 'un," replied Flatnose as he used his flint and steel to light the campfire.

"Whooee, those mules are stirring up a heap of mud," reported Gutsy, as he handed Cookie two pails of clean water.

"Best we try to get them out," said Petre. "We're not too far from the quicksand bar. Besides, if the Comanches are going to camp near here, they'll need clean water."

"If we're going to eat their stew, we sure want them to have clean water," said Rocky. "Where's that bell?"

"Think you can be old Bess?" asked Gutsy.

"Here's the bell, but you'll probably need a whip to crack over their heads," said Cookie, who was preparing the coffee and buffalo steaks. "Hurry, it'll be time for story telling as soon as this meat is finished."

"Here, Gutsy, you're the best bell ringer, next to old Bess. You stay on this side of the river and ring, while me and Petre will go up stream and cross the river and try to drive them back. Bible John and Flatnose kin come in from downstream side. That ought to bring them back here," said Rocky.

"Jeb has already started to put the stakes into the ground. When the mules git here, loop a rope around their necks and send them on to Jeb," said Bible John. "If you are lucky, old Bess will come first and you will be able to lead them."

"Look smart as you ring that bell," cautioned Petre. "They're so frisky they may just sweep you away with them."

"I'll drive stakes with Jeb," said Doc.

He hurried away to help.

"Where's the feast to be?" Doc asked Jeb.

"Don't know yet. Here somewhere, but if we stake the mules close to our camp, we'll be better able to watch."

"Never been to an Indian feast before," muttered Doc, as he hammered a stake into the ground.

"Well, one thing you must do is be careful. This one will be a mite different because of Gutsy, but watch yourself and don't upset them" cautioned Jeb. "Say, have you ever eaten buffalo meat before?"

"Yes, on the trip over from Philadelphia," answered Doc between whacks on the stake.

"Was it stewed?" asked Jeb.

"Some of it was; but I've eaten it fried and roasted, too," answered Doc.

"Then you won't have any trouble; but, remember, you must eat whatever is offered—with a smile," instructed Jeb.

"Good thing my stomach is better. This trip has almost made me well," said Doc.

"Noticed that, Doc. by the time we get to Cerrillos, you'll be ready to make other people well," said Jeb.

"Speaking of that, I'd like to be Gutsy's guardian or whatever it is called in this area. I'll set up practice, and I'll be able to care for him," Doc said.

"Even if you don't make any more money, you've got plenty now, eh, Doc?" Jeb grinned as he said that.

"What makes you say that?" asked Doc with a startled look on his face.

"When I take on the responsibility of a man's life as I did yours, I make it my business to know what he's carrying. You're carrying plenty," said Jeb.

"Enough to set up practice and help a young boy," answered Doc.

"Well, Gutsy will have to decide. He's pretty independent," Jeb said.

"Smart, too. His hands are shaped just right to make a good surgeon," added Doc.

"Yippee kyii, yiii, yiii!" yelled Petre, as he cracked his whip in the air.

"Yippee ki yi yi," yelled Bible John, as Flatnose cracked his whip in the air from the other direction.

"Look smart there, Gutsy," called Cookie. "Ring that bell hard."

No one knew if the whip frightened them; if the bell enticed them, or if they had enough water and wanted to eat grass and rest. Whatever the cause, the mules formed a line behind old Bess and calmly trotted to the night stakes where six pairs of hands made them fast for the night.

"Come and get it! Come and get it!" called Cookie. "Take a cup, fill your plate, and let's hear the stories of this afternoon's work. Here, Flatnose, have a part of your special tongue. Betcha it's better than Flower With Any Colored Face can fix."

"Give us all some, Cookie, and we'll help him decide," said Jeb. "Doc, you'd better taste this—you may have some presented to you."

First, let's talk about the feast," urged Gutsy. "I've never been to one."

"Your first one, and you're the star attraction," said Rocky.

"What?" asked Gutsy.

"Yep, tonight you are to become a Comanche," said Bible John.

"Turning Red is to become your blood brother," chortled Petre. "Must be a real sacrifice for him, 'cause now he'll have even more white blood in his body.

"Maybe he doesn't hate his white blood," Doc said, "only what has happened to him because of it."

"Tell you what. Those squaws will have to be real good to beat this food," said Jeb.

"Best tongue I ever ate," added Bible John.

"What did I tell you, Flatnose?" crowed Cookie.

"It's mighty fine," agreed Flatnose, "but the real reason I chose this train to travel with is your coffee. It plumb takes the tucker out of my tuck."

"He's right, Cookie," said Doc. "I'll probably never enjoy regular coffee again."

"Regular! This is regular. Ain't no dishwater like you'll get in Cerrillos," snorted Cookie. "Now just how many buffalo did you kill?"

"Turning Red said we killed seventy-two; the braves had only bows and arrows, but they still shot over twenty," said Jeb.

"My Gawd! Ninety-two buffaloes," exclaimed Cookie.

"Yeah. Jeb selected three for us," said Rocky. "We wanted to clean them and bring them along, but since we won the contest, Turning Red sent us on with this hump and the special tongue.

"Said they'd give us the rest later, after the squaws had made it ready," finished Petre.

"Those squaws have my sympathy. Can you imagine cleaning over ninety of them old humped-back cows?" exclaimed Cookie.

"How many women were there?" asked Doc.

"Mebbe fifty or sixty. Turning Red said Swiftly Running Feet would fix the hides for us," answered Flatnose.

"We agreed to stay here a couple of days and rest our mules," explained Jeb.

"Do you think they'll let us leave?" asked Cookie.

"Of course they will. Turning Red won't let anyone hurt us," said Gutsy.

After all, we'll have the newest Comanche with us. You still will stay with us white men, won't you?" Petre said.

"How much is your contract with Mister Barnes?" asked Doc.

"It was two hundred dollars when it started,' said Gutsy. "I've worked two years and three months, but I'm not very good. Old Barnes made us pay for anything we ruined, and he said I have more against me than I have earned."

"We'll find out about that. Before you pay one red cent, we'll have an accounting from that man," said Jeb.

"You all believe I can do it, don't you?" asked Gutsy.

"Darn tooting you can," said Cookie. "Don't you worry one minute! Only one thing I want is to be there when you hand old Barnes his money. By gum, I'll betchee he'll look like an old lobo timber wolf eating sour persimmons."

"But why? asked Gutsy. "After all, he'll have his money."

"Yeah, but what he won't have is a darned good saddler in slavery," said Cookie.

"Listen! What's that noise?" asked Doc.

"Must be the first of the Injuns. I hope their horses don't stampede in this direction. Cookie, if they come here, do we have enough grub to feed them something?" asked Jeb.

Cookie nodded his head.

"Remember, not one word about whiskey, Bible John!" ordered Jeb.

"Been around whiskey and Injuns. I know better than to say anything," muttered Bible John.

"Well, see to it you remember it the entire time. If you forget, you can be sure I never will," said Jeb.

About five minutes downstream, by foot, was a clearing where the bands of Comanches camped year after year to prepare their meat for the winter. Because it was one of their migratory homes, they always used the same hooks made from branches of the trees to hang the meat away from wild animals. This year, willing hands prepared many new branches to take care of the largest kill they had ever had.

Women hauled heavy travois, loaded with meat and hides, to the camp. Older men, no longer hunters, dragged travois behind their horses. A second and third trip were made before dark. Every scrap of meat was brought to the camp.

The hearts, those not eaten raw on the field, were cleaned and brought in first. They were prepared for the hunters, because this tribe believed a hunter's strength was increased by that of the animal if that organ was eaten. After the entire tribe, this time including the women, children and old men, had eaten, fifty hearts remained to be served at the feast.

The livers, another great prize, raw or cooked, were loaded together, brought to the camp for the feast and to be prepared for the winter.

The huge intestines were emptied and carried to the camp to be washed. Later they would be filled and used as water bags for their long, hot journeys. The smaller guts were included in a specialty dish, served to the entire tribe.

The heads were left for the wild animals and carrion birds to feast on for the next several days. Later the women would return and remove the horns, which they would use for cooking implements and decorations.

The tendons of the legs were cured and used as twine. Some laced moccasins together, some strapped pack on the travois or the pack animals.

Because Indians lived off the land, they learned to use everything. They were the first to use buffalo droppings to make campfires. This information was passed from the Indians to the trappers and on to travelers, saving the lives of many people.

For the feast, a huge fire was built in the center of the camp. Each woman had her own special small fire. Each took turns working at the big central fire for the community feast, while on her own fire she prepared her specialty. Competition ran high at the feasts, each older woman carefully protected her status as cook. The younger ones tried to win the title of being the best feast maker away from the older women.

Swiftly Running Feet hurried her preparations; she had her prized duty of preparing the three hides. Her heart sang. Turning Red had chosen her to prepare the bed robe for his blood brother. It was a great honor to be chosen to prepare these skins for the mule train, but even more to prepare one for the soon-to-be blood brother of the leading brave.

It must mean that Turning Red, the bravest of their braves, considered her to be the best woman in their tribe. Maybe, she hoped fervently in her secret heart, he favored her above all others for himself. She resolved to make these hides beautiful, even better than those in her own permanent wickiup back in the forest. She would prove how skilled she was, and maybe this fall Turning Red would choose her as his woman.

"It's strange," Swiftly Running Feet said to her mother, "that he would have more interest in this white boy than he has in me."

"If you want to be the woman of a white man, you must expect many strange things," replied her mother. "I'll help you prepare the same special heart dish for him that I prepared for your father. This should show him you admire his strength and courage. You must also treat his brother as you would Turning Red. That act will prove you accept his entire family."

"I'll do all these things, but so will many other girls," said Swiftly Running Feet.

"Ah, yes," replied Happy Eyes, "but no one else has been asked to prepare the hides."

Swiftly Running Feet's heart sang. It was true, she had been the one chosen. Her mother must be correct. She knew her mother was considered to be the wisest old woman in the entire tribe, therefore she would believe what she said. She would be friendly and helpful and hopeful.

Rhea Coleman

Wickiup

SEVEN

After the last clinging finger of the sun had been unclasped and it had gone unhindered on its way toward the beckoning west, Flatnose returned quietly to the team's camp.

"See you got the mules all safe and sound behind their packs," he commented.

"Did you see Turning Red?" asked Gutsy. "Is the feast ready?"

"Didn't see your friend, but everything seems fine. Your soon-to-be family is too gol darned busy to be up to any mischief," answered Flatnose.

"See, I told you, when Turning Red makes a promise, he means it," said Gutsy proudly.

"Appears to be, Gutsy, appears to be. Where be the rest of the hosses?"

"Each one is staked in a different spot, just in case," replied Rocky.

"Wall, now, probably don't hurt, but if those Injuns mean mischief, none of us'll live to need those hosses," said Flatnose. "I'm inclined to believe Gutsy. If he's right, we're eight lucky humans."

"If we make friends with this tribe and keep it, we'll never have to worry about the safety on this section of the trail," said Jeb.

"We have their friendship, Turning Red said so," exclaimed Gutsy.

"You have their friendship; we are alive only because you're with us," said Bible John, "and I, for one, am grateful. Never did fancy arrow holes in my body, nor having an Injun lift my hair."

"Our best bet is to go to the feast and be on our best behavior. I'd like to live to set up practice in Cerrillos," said Doc.

"Hey now, Doc, that's an idea. Maybe you could heal some of the Injuns and make friends that way," suggested Petre.

"And mebbe get us killed, if the medicine man disagrees," said Rocky.

"In that case, I'll wait until Turning Red asks me," said Doc.

"Hey, something is smelling good. I almost taste it way over here," sniffed Petre.

"Probably it's one of those buffaloes being roasted whole," answered Rocky.

"Say, Cookie, what do you have packed up there?" asked Doc.

"Some coffee. Thought I'd offer to make some if they want it," replied Cookie.

"Good idee! What are you taking as a gift, Flatnose?" asked Jeb.

"Wal, squaws work so hard, I'm taking two Green River knives."

"How come people say, up to the Green River, when they cut deep?" asked Gutsy.

"Lots of people think it means the river, but it don't. Means the knife is in past its brand name," said Flatnose, chuckling.

"I'm going to write that in my log. People back east will be glad to have that puzzle solved," exclaimed Doc. He chuckled too.

"What have you got, Rocky and Petre?" asked Jeb.

"We're traveling light, but we each have an extry flint and steel. Thought we'd show off an easy way to make a fire and give these to their chief," explained Petre.

Jeb nodded in agreement.

"Nothing like the holy word—I intend to give them a couple of Bibles," said Bible John.

"Do you suppose the medicine man would be able to use any of my supplies?" asked Doc.

"Do you have anything for a hangover?" asked Bible John, his laugh wasn't as innocent as he pretended.

"No more of that!" roared Jeb.

"What about a surgical knife? Like the one you used to lance my boil?" suggested Cookie.

"Surely, if you think it's a good idea," said Doc.

"Yep, the one with the two little points on the end, like devil's horns," suggested Rocky. His joke and laugh wasn't that innocent either.

"Maybe a pair of scissors?" asked Doc.

"That's exactly it!" exclaimed Flatnose. "Mebbe they've never seen any such things, so you'll have to explain how to use them, but scissors are a good idea."

"How about you, Jeb? What are you taking?" asked Cookie.

"Thought I'd take a bag of sugar from our supply. Nothing like easing a sweet tooth," replied Jeb.

"Great! We can spare it, and I've never seen anyone turn down a treat like that. Let's go, I'm plumb antsy," Cookie said.

"But what about me? asked Gutsy. "I don't have any kind of gift."

"Come on—you're the guest of honor. You don't need a gift," explained Flatnose.

The men and Gutsy quietly made their way to the Indian encampment; however, they did not surprise the natives. During the time Flatnose had scouted the Indians, the Indians had scouted the team's camp. One ran swiftly ahead to tell the chief when the group left for the feast.

As they arrived, the newcomers were greeted and taken immediately to a place among the many braves who were waiting around a small ceremonial fire. Gutsy was given a special place beside Chief Searching Truth, who was adorned with his feather bonnet and many necklaces, bracelets and anklets. The space on the chief's other side was vacant.

Jeb, Flatnose, Petre, Rocky, and Cookie were each seated between two warrior braves.

Doc was taken before a masked man who danced around him, shaking rattles in both hands. Doc stood straight and very still. He was trying to memorize everything about this spectacle so he could include it in his journal. He was too startled and interested to move.

The masked man struck Doc on the right shoulder; he then went into many spins and leaps, each one seeming higher and faster than the last. He turned and circled Doc in the other direction, striking him on the left shoulder as he continued to leap, spin, and whirl.

Doc, in shock, stood and waited. The masked man picked up burning firebrands and threw them at Doc; none were actually meant to hit Doc, and they did not.

Doc, still frozen in his tracks, waited.

Gradually, the frenzied dancing stopped. The masked man walked over to the blazing logs; he took off his mask and threw it into the fire. His face reflected horror as he watched it burn. Next he took his rattles and necklaces and threw them into the fire; they burned.

He started another dance, but stopped as Chief Searching Truth stood tall and walked over to the two men, motioning them to sit together near the center of the circle. The now unmasked medicine man hesitated. Doc, able to move once again, quickly took his seat, wondering what would happen next.

Chief Searching Truth returned to his seat. He gestured with his right hand, and a brave brought the filled ceremonial pipe and placed it in the outstretched hand. Carefully the chief drew on the pipe as another brave held a glowing ember to the tobacco. When Chief Searching Truth was satisfied the pipe would stay lit, he passed it to Gutsy. Gutsy drew manfully on the pipe, managing to hold only a little in his lungs which he blew out to show his friendship. Quickly he passed the pipe to his right.

Not a word was spoken as each man in the circle took his turn and passed the pipe on. Because the circle was large, it was necessary for the chief to fill the bowl and start it again before all the braves had their turns.

The third time Chief Searching Truth prepared the pipe, he carried it to the two men of medicine seated in the center. He took the long ceremonial draw before he passed it to Doc, who was prepared to participate in the ritual because he had watched the others. Doc drew deeply, gathered the smoke in his lungs and released it slowly. Gravely, he returned the sacred red granite pipe to Chief Searching Truth, who handed it to the unmasked medicine man.

The Indian medicine man refused the pipe by pretending not to notice it was his turn. The chief rattled one of his necklaces and again handed the pipe to the medicine man. The chief and the medicine man glared at each other. The unmasked man haughtily took the pipe, drew quickly, released a little smoke, and handed back the pipe as if it burned his hand. With great dignity the chief returned to his place.

Seated in the formerly vacant spot at the other side of Chief Searching Truth was Turning Red. Obviously, he had just returned from a journey.

Carefully, the chief cleared the still-burning tobacco from the sacred pipe. He dug a hole in the sand and placed the unused tobacco into it.

For a fourth time, he motioned to the brave to bring more tobacco and reload the pipe. Turning Red was given the pipe first. After his turn, he immediately went to the center and presented the pipe to Doc and next to the medicine man. This time the pipe was accepted and Turning Red returned to his seat after he passed the pipe to the others in the circle.

After the circle had finished the round, Chief Searching Truth spoke briefly, waiting for Turning Red to translate for the benefit of the American speaking guests.

"Tonight we celebrate three great events," translated Turning Red. "First, because of the help of our friends, who used their fire sticks to help us, we have an ample supply of food to face the winter. Even if we have many guests we will have meat for all.

"Second, we have witnessed two men of medicine, even though of very different training, smoke the peace pipe. This is good. We will all gain when each shares his knowledge with the other.

"Third, we are here to unite two great races, the red and the white. Turning Red, our bravest brave, has told us of the courage of Gutsy and his past kindness to him. We are happy to know this, and we are proud to make him our brother by blood. Please, would both of you come before me and we will seal this pact."

Gutsy and Turning Red held out their right arms. Chief Searching Truth, using a sharpened bone, cut into the vein of each, and placed the wrists together so their flowing blood would mingle. He bound their wrists together with a piece of soft white doeskin. He motioned to the other warriors and they stood; he motioned for the white men to join the braves in the circle.

The drummer started a slow beat, and the chief led the entire circle, including Doc and the medicine man in a dance. First the drumbeats were even and slow so the white men could learn the step, shuffle, step of the dance. Then the drummer picked up the beat gradually until they were dancing at a wild, breathtaking pace. Abruptly the drum stopped.

As if this were a signal the women of the tribe rushed in and the drum resumed its rhythmical beat, faster and faster. The dance became a matter of survival for the white men, but an expression of health and vigor for the braves and squaws.

The music stopped and the chief removed the doeskin leather from the young men's forearms, cut it in two pieces, and presented one to each blood brother, saying, "Just as this symbol can be completely whole only when it is together, so will your spirits be. In kindness to your spirits be together often."

Even Flatnose had suspiciously shiny eyes. Next, the brothers were seated together and each was served a bowl of broth.

"We are each to sip from our own bowl, exchange it, and finish what is left from the other's bowl," whispered Turning Red.

"This is good soup. I'm glad to share it with you," answered Gutsy.

Turning Red translated the compliment to the cooks; the women giggled happily. Swiftly Running Feet brought the specially prepared heart dish. She turned as if she were going to serve Turning Red first.

Before he could ask her to serve Gutsy, she said, "It warms my heart to give this special food to our brother. Welcome, Brother," she whispered as she served Gutsy and quickly backed away.

"Do we exchange this, also?" asked Gutsy.

"Yes, part of it. It symbolizes that we will both have the same brave heart and receive the same strength from the animal world. If it is difficult for you, eat only a small amount for your portion and I will eat the rest, offered Turning Red.

"Thank you. It is strange to me," said Gutsy.

"Here come the first cuts from the roasted buffalo. We are to give each other the finest piece. This symbolizes that we place the other's wishes above our own. Do you have a preference?" asked Turning Red.

"No, I like it all; but if you give me a little of your preference, I'll give that piece from my plate to you," answered Gutsy.

Both brothers finished eating their portions of the buffalo prepared by the women of the tribe.

"We have fulfilled the ritual now. We are free to do as we wish. What will be your first deed as a Comanche?" asked Turning Red.

Before Gutsy could reply, Turning Red said, "But, first tell me what happened between the medicine man and Doc?"

"The chief made them smoke the peace pipe," answered Gutsy.

"I saw that, but why was Elifi without his mask?" asked Turning Red.

"He threw it into the fire," explained Gutsy.

"Did he do anything to Doc first?" asked Turning Red.

"He danced and shook and whirled and struck Doc on each shoulder with his rattles," answered Gutsy.

"What did Doc do?" asked Turning Red.

"He didn't know what to do, so he just stood there. What should he have done?" asked Gutsy.

"He did the right thing. Elifi was trying to prove his medicine was stronger than Doc's," said Turning Red in explanation.

"Oh, so when Doc didn't move, it proved Doc's was stronger?" asked Gutsy.

"Yes, and probably the reason it worked was the poor doctor was so scared he couldn't move," chuckled Turning Red.

"I don't know about Doc, but I was. That's for sure," admitted Gutsy.

"If I weren't half Indian, raised each summer in the tribe, I would have been, too," agreed Turning Red.

People were beginning to move away from the roasted buffalo, even though almost half remained to be eaten.

"Looks as if everyone's had his fill for the moment. Now comes more fun. It's gift-giving time," explained Turning Red.

"I won't enjoy this, I don't have a gift. All I have to my name is what I have on, and nobody would want that," said Gutsy.

"You've already given your gift. Now I must translate. I see your cook is going to be first," whispered Turning Red.

"In honor of the three celebrations, I would like to present this coffee. Also, if you like, I will make some for the feast," announced Cookie.

"Cookie, in the name of the Chief Searching Truth we accept with pleasure. The fame of your coffee has preceded you. If you need anything, the women will lend a hand," responded Turning Red.

"Only things I need are water and a big pan. Seems to be plenty of both right here," answered Cookie.

Long Stride, cousin of Turning Red, was next. "The family of Turning Red would like to present to our new family member a buckskin, with the story of his family drawn upon it," announced Long Stride.

"How beautiful, Turning Red. Please tell my family how proud of it I am," responded Gutsy.

"Actually you will receive it tomorrow, because the story of this feast must be added," Turning Red explained, after translating Gutsy's words to the rest.

"I'm so excited I can't stand still," whispered Gutsy.

"I see Jeb wants to speak next. What does he bring?" asked Turning Red.

"Sugar," responded Gutsy.

"Very wise. For some, it'll be their first taste; our sweet is honey or sometimes sap from plants," said Turning Red.

"Chief, may I present to you and to your people these sweet crystals?" asked Jeb, and he sat down.

"These are part of the magic of the white man," explained Turning Red. "They are difficult to get and come from far, far away. If you put a few grains on something sour, it will change the taste to sweet. Even sour fruit can be changed with these crystals."

He placed a few grains on the palm of the chief's hand and asked him to taste. The delight on Searching Truth's face was enough to convince all they were seeing another evidence of the cleverness of the white man.

Another new cousin, Laughing Bear, asked to present a gift.

"We understand you are going over the land of heat below and sun above. You may need to find the water that runs below the heated sands. Here are two magic stick that will help you," said Laughing Bear.

"Thank you, Cousin. Tomorrow, will you show me just how to use them?" asked Gutsy.

"We'll both give you lessons tomorrow," said Turning Red after he had translated Gutsy's answer.

"Petre and Rocky have something for you," said Flatnose, "but they need a little wood to demonstrate it."

A young boy was sent for some twigs. Petre broke the twigs even smaller and stacked them carefully. Rocky struck the flint against the steel to make sparks. The sparks landed on the dry twigs and made a fire. Only Turning Red had used these before; the rest gaped in amazement.

Petre and Rocky each presented one to the chief, saying one was for the hunters and one for the home camp. Wonderingly, the chief accepted the magic of the fire makers. He was glad the old problem of someone carrying fire wherever they traveled was solved. His gratitude was reflected on his usually stoic face.

The mother of Turning Red took her turn. She had made new water sacks from the long intestines of the freshly killed buffaloes; she presented one to each traveler.

The travelers graciously accepted the water sacks, which she had cleaned and blown up with air to keep the sides separated until they were filled with water.

Flatnose, afraid the others would not understand, jumped up to add his thanks to Gutsy's. "The first time I saw that type of water bag wrapped around a horse, I thought something was the matter—a strange health problem. But when we were thirsty and hot and tired, and a long way from water, I learned how handy these are. Thank you from all of us."

He bowed gallantly toward Turning Red's mother.

"Now, before I sit down, I'd like to present a gift to help your squaws. These are knives that can be sharpened again and again, by using this stone."

Flatnose started to explain.

"Those look like Green Rivers," interrupted Turning Red.

"That's right," answered Flatnose.

"Brothers and sisters, these are the finest knives. My father sells them, but only to his white trappers. No Indian would be allowed to buy this quality, no matter how many furs you offered; but, Flatnose, your friend, has presented two to our tribe. Thank you, Flatnose," said Turning Red. "Now my uncle has a gift for his new nephew."

"Once, many moons ago, a white man came to our village. He rode a great red horse and on it was this saddle. None of my family ever used this kind, but now I have a white man as a nephew I would like to present him with this saddle," said Turning Red, translating.

"Thank you, Uncle. This is the kind of saddle I could use. Look, it was even made at Barnes Saddle Shop. He might not be pleased I have it, but I am. Thank you again, Uncle," exclaimed Gutsy.

"Bible John has a gift for our tribe," whispered Gutsy.

"Hope it's those two Bibles he's holding," Turning Red said, as Bible John stepped forward and presented them to the chief.

"But, you said you didn't believe in the Bible," remonstrated Gutsy.

"Don't, but the special parchment used for the pages is very strong, and the warriors like to put some between the two skins on their shields. It protects them, even if not exactly the way Bible John teaches.

"Now it's the women's turn. They want to thank our friends for the bountiful supply of buffalo meat. Not only will the meat supply our tribe for a long time, but the skins will warm us even longer," announced Turning Red.

Happy Eyes had been chosen to present the gifts. One for each man's horse and one for each of the thirty-nine mules.

She said, "Please accept these new saddle blankets and pieces of fur to ease the burdens of your animals. May you ride these prairies in peace all your years."

"Thank you. Thank you. These are wonderful. Feel how soft they are, these old animals of our'n are sure lucky," responded Jeb. He smiled as he ran his hands over each one.

"What's the matter, Gutsy? Trying to figure how to carry all your gifts?" asked Turning Red.

"Yes. Guess I'll just have to lade a mule or two a little higher," answered Gutsy.

"To my fellow worker in preserving the health of mankind, I wish to make a small gift of this pair of surgical scissors," said Doc, holding out the gift toward Elifi.

Rapidly Turning Red translated. He explained the magic of the double knife. He demonstrated how easily and smoothly it cut. Even the jealous medicine man was pleased, and accepted willingly.

"Perhaps tomorrow you can help us talk about our work," suggested Doc to Turning Red.

"I would like to know more of your magic," said Elifi, agreeing after it was translated to him.

"Turning Red tells me your magic is so strong it can cure a problem we have here. We all ask your help."

"It would be my greatest pleasure," answered Doc.

"Good. Now we have come to the exchange of gifts between brothers, and first I want to show you the gift my brother gave me," announced Turning Red.

"About two years ago, when I first realized I could not be a white man, I ran away from the school where I was studying law—white man's law. I liked law until I learned I was not a man, but a savage. Only because my father wished to give them to me did I have any of the white man's rights. I became angry and I ran away. I went to Old Barnes to buy a saddle. I had money, but my high cheekbones and coloring made him decide the money was stolen and he chased me with a club. Gutsy hid me in a shed.

"I heard him threaten Gutsy, and I heard the sound of the whip as he used it on Gutsy. Gutsy had locked the shed from the outside, so I could not help him. After Barnes was too tired to whip any more, he went to bed. Gutsy came, opened the shed door so I could go away. He gave me a bowl of soup and a piece of dried bread, I'm sure it was his only supper. Now, Gutsy, please remove your shirt," said Turning Red.

"Oh, I can't do that," said Gutsy, clutching his shirt to keep it down.

"Then I will help you," said Turning Red,

"No, please, no," pleaded Gutsy, as Turning Red removed the shirt and pointed to his back.

"There! See those scars? Not the new ones, but the permanent old ones—see those? That's my little brother's gift to me."

Gutsy stood with his head down as he said, "But if he hadn't whipped me for that, he would have found something else."

"But he did whip you because of me, and you did receive these scars because of me," said Turning Red.

"I've asked Gutsy to live with us, but he feels he must go on to Cerrillos and earn money to pay Barnes for his contract," Turning Red continued, "If he doesn't, his little brother will have to take his place. This is his choice, but, so he won't have to walk all the way to Cerrillos, I returned to our camp this afternoon and brought Big Red back for him."

Gutsy's mouth dropped open. No word passed his lips, he was truly speechless.

Turning Red laughed, he pretended to think the reason Gutsy was speechless was because he was afraid of the horse.

"Little brother, he looks big, I know, but you will grow up to him. Right now, because he is trained for trick riding, he'll accept you as the rider even with shortened stirrups. He's a son of the horse who carried the owner of your saddle. Note that his ears are split. This proves he's a Comanche horse," explained Turning Red.

"But I can't take your special horse," Gutsy said.

"Then I can't accept your whipping," interrupted Turning Red.

"You have to, it's all in the past," said Gutsy.

So is my ownership of this horse. It's not mine anymore—I have given it to you. Here, give me the new saddle blanket and a piece of buffalo hide. Now let me have your new saddle. That looks pretty good, but what about the bridle, the bit, and the reins?" asked Turning Red.

He put his hand on his chin and pretending to be thinking.

"Here, please present my gift," said Chief Searching Truth. "I'm proud to have the newest member of my tribe using my old reins. I also want to say, that any time you want to live with our family there is a space in my wickiup."

Once again Gutsy's mouth moved up and down; still he could speak no words.

"Step into my hand, little brother. I'll help you up and I'll walk with you to your camp. It'll do me good to see those other white men walking and you riding a spirited Indian trained horse."

Hogbacks — *Rhea Coleman*

EIGHT

C ain't live like this," grumbled Jeb. "For one, I'll be glad to be on our way tomorrow."

"Hooray," said Rocky. "I've eaten enough squaw food to last the next nine week."

"Me, too. I know this'll split Cookie's head, but his cooking is more my style," said Flatnose.

"Yep, we'd better take Flatnose out of here, else he'll be carrying a squaw along, and I'll have to teach her how to cook," grumbled Cookie.

"Ain't so," snorted Flatnose. "Made it these many years by myself, reckon I'll get along as many more as the good Lawd gives me."

"Now he's started spouting religion as well as poetry. He's hopeless," Rocky laughed.

"Dry up," said Flatnose. "I'm packing to leave tomorrow early, be you?"

"The mule's packs are ready, lined in the right order; the horses fed, watered, and curried; the water containers, including those given us by the Indians, are filled and ready," said Petre. "Right now, all we need is Gutsy and his hoss."

"Guess he'll never tire of it. He's brushed and curried that hoss until it glows," said Cookie. "But he's done his share of getting ready, so he can have a little fun." By now, to Cookie, Gutsy could do no wrong.

Jeb felt the same way. He said, "He's saved our bacons enough times that even if he didn't help, he'd be welcome on this train."

"He's the luckiest one kid I've ever seen. Hope it keeps up until we get to Cerrillos," agreed Petre.

Yiiiiieeeee!" called Gutsy as he rode into camp. He threw the reins forward over Lucky's head as the horse stopped and lowered it's head, and Gutsy slid to the ground.

"Newest trick—pretty sharp, don't you think?" Gutsy asked proudly.

"Don't tell me he's like a camel and kneels so you can climb on his back." Cookie pretended to growl, he didn't want Gutsy to know how he felt about him.

"Not yet. But he holds real still when I take a kind of running jump and land where I'm supposed to. You people forget that I'm fourteen years old and almost a man," answered Gusty.

"Don't you be doing that," said Flatnose. "Here, I fixed you a rope ladder that'll hang from your saddle horn. When you don't need it, you can wrap it around."

"So that's what he's been weaving. Hump, guess my offer to help you whenever you needed it isn't necessary," grumbled Cookie jealously.

"Let's get Lucky staked and try to sleep," said Jeb, putting a stop to the bickering. "show us how you unsaddle your hoss."

"Turning Red showed me. I just uncinch and pull, it's easy to do. I've knocked myself over once or maybe twice. But I can do it now. Thanks, Flatnose, for the rope ladder, though. I know I'll have a lot of use for it," said Gutsy.

"Can you get him to put his head down so you can put the bridle on him?" asked Rocky.

"He's patient, and I'm learning," admitted Gutsy.

"Well, never mind, we'll all be here in the mornings," said Cookie.

"Thanks, and thanks for not laughing at me because it takes longer for me to get him ready," said Gutsy.

"Why, Gutsy, I'd be afraid to make fun of you for fear you'll soon be six foot five and look down on me," exclaimed Doc.

"Thanks, Doc," grinned Gutsy. "Now I'd better fix my bed, with my saddle for my head like you men do; after I stake Lucky, of course."

"You'd think he was forty, not fourteen," muttered Jeb to Cookie.

Gutsy was sure he had not been asleep when Cookie shook him and whispered, "Let's get going. Morning's just over there, and we need coffee boiling and bread baking before it gets here."

"Why are the horses so restless?" whispered Gutsy as soon as he sat up.

"Don't know for sure, but I think your friends are all around us," answered Cookie.

"They've probably come to help," answered Gutsy.

"Gol darn, I hope you're right," said Cookie with great fervor.

"What's first?" asked Gutsy.

"Give them beans a stir, then bring the hosses around. Best do your trick of pouring water on the mule stakes, too," ordered Cookie.

By the time the stakes were ready to be pulled, the other men had the horses saddled and were ready to start loading the mules.

"First, old Bess," said Jeb. "The others will follow better."

"Sure gives you the creeps, knowing the Injuns are everywhere, but cain't see a one," whispered Rocky.

"Just keep loading," said Jeb. "We'll take turns eating so the team won't be alone."

"Don't want much food, but need some of that good coffee," said Flatnose as he packed still another mule.

In less than an hour, thirty-nine eager-to-go mules were ready, each in his proper place, waiting impatiently for Cookie to lead out.

After breakfast, the bread for the next four days was wrapped and put on top of four different mules; the beans were drained and put on top of four more. Cooked buffalo meat was packed the same way, but only for two days; the last two days of the trip across the cutoff the crew would have to eat dried meat. Cookie wrapped his buffalo gut full of water over and around the second day's meat, hoping to protect if from the blazing sun of the desert.

Meals prepared, Cookie took one last look around, put his right leg over old Bess, sat in his saddle, checked the train, and drew in his breath. Everywhere he looked he saw there were Comanches. The same friendly Comanches of the feast days; but every one knew the feast days were over.

Turning Red rode toward Jeb and said, "We're here to help you cross the Arkansas. The quicksand is just to your right. You may have problems."

"Thank you," Jeb quickly answered.

He turned to the team and yelled, "Come on there, Cookie. Give old Bess her kick; Gutsy, lead out that prancing new hoss, but don't let him run. Let's get this misbegotten business on the road! Turning Red, Call your braves aside and give us room as we start our trip across this hellish land! Cookie, give Bess another kick. Whap her a bit—she's lazy from the two day's rest. Whooee, old Bess get a move on, start that bell ringing. We got people expecting us in Cerrillos. Begone! Begone, I say. If you want to rest tonight, you'd better cross that muddy river."

Slowly they crossed. The team waded in single file between two rows of whooping Indians astride prancing ponies. The two scouts were ahead; Jeb and Flatnose brought up the rear, prepared for any strange movements. As the last mule climbed the banks to safety and followed into the hot dry sand of the desert, Turning Red hurried forward to Gutsy.

"Here, brother, is your buffalo meat, your hides, and the ceremonial skin. This pack horse is yours. You need it now to carry your belongings. Remember, you have a home, always. I'll ride close to you and drop the pack horse's reins over your saddle horn. That way she'll make the transfer easily," explained Turning Red.

"Holding up his right wrist to show the scar of the ceremony, Turning Red added: "You might want to tell Jeb it's easier to travel at night across this area. It will be almost a full moon for the four or five nights you'll be traveling the desert, so it will be light enough. Good-bye, Brother. We'll meet again, soon."

"Good-bye, Brother. Thanks for everything. I'll take good care of Lucky and the other horse, too," Gutsy said, as he held up his own right wrist.

He successfully managed the three reins, the lead rope for the mule train, Lucky's reins, and now the gift pack horse.

"Oh, his name is Spook, if you want to use it." Turning Red whirled his horse toward the Arkansas and each brave followed his example like a well-trained cavalry unit.

"Glad to see them go," muttered Rocky. "I know Gutsy is as good as a Comanche, but I feel better with them gone."

"Let's go by and help the kid with that extry hoss," said Petre.

"Want us to put the extry hoss to the back?" asked Rocky as they rode alongside.

"Yes, I'm just starting to get used to the two sets of reins. I'm not good enough to handle three," answered Gutsy.

"You're doing great, but this one will travel better hitched behind," said Petre.

"Come on, Cookie, let's speed up a bit. We want to stop before the sun gets too hot and give the animals a rest. Let's give them a little run now, while it's kinda cool," called Jeb.

Everyone enjoyed stretching their legs. Their life was movement and they had been still too long; nothing felt so good as heading out across unmarked plains or deserts.

Long before the sun was halfway up the sky, Jeb called, "Circle up, circle up!"

Petre, the head scout, led the team to the shade of a sand dune. The mules were unloaded. The men piled the packs high before stretching skins from stack to stack, making as much shade as possible. The mules and horses crowded beneath the shelter.

Flatnose unwrapped one of the water containers and watered the animals; Gutsy fed a little gramma grass to each animal. The animals settled peacefully into their standing *siesta.*

Gutsy unpacked the packhorse's load. He found his ceremonial hide, to which had been added the story of the tribal ceremony making him the blood brother of Turning Red. There were two extra hides ready to be made into moccasins, enough smoked and cured buffalo meat for the rest of the journey, and the buffalo hide to put under him at night for his bed. Also he found four long sticks and seven skins sewed together, so they could be attached to the sticks and stretched out as a shelter from the fiercely burning sun.

Even though the morning had been short, the men were glad to stop and take their own *siesta.*

"Doc, what do you think of this noon *siesta?*" asked Bible John.

"Before I had thought it was just a poor joke, but here I can see it is necessary," answered Doc.

"Yep, usually this is the time when the tallest tales are told, the best plans made, and if you feel like it, a little sleep is fine, too," said Rocky.

"Speaking of plans, you might want to know that during this stage of the trip we will be traveling at night. The moon is getting on to full; we will have plenty of light. The desert is cold at night, but we will be exercising, so a light jacket will be all that is necessary," said Jeb.

Gutsy glowed with pride; both his brother and his hero knew about traveling in this land. He slept during the allotted *siesta* break.

"Water's so hot we could almost make fresh coffee," grumbled Petre.

"Heard it said you can fry an egg on a rock, if you can find a rock." Cookie laughed.

"How about setting a pan of water in the sand?" asked Gutsy, awakening from his *siesta*.

We can use a couple of sticks of wood Gutsy packed, to boil the coffee, but the beans don't need heating, and we have meat and bread," said Cookie.

"Don't get out in the heat," said Jeb. "Eat things as they are. We'll wait another two hours before starting to load. Right now the sand would burn the animals' feet and cause your moccasins to crack. By tomorrow, we'll have to tie pads on the animals' feet before we start."

"No wonder Indians call this the land of heat below and sun above," said Flatnose.

"White men have a name for it too, they call it Hell," said Rocky.

"Three more days and we should be through it," explained Jeb. "Say, Doc, I believe you're melting away."

"I'm thinner, if that's what you mean, but I'm enjoying the heat. Cooks the poisons out of a body, you know. Certainly, I'm one who can vouch for that. If I get much better I won't be able to control myself," said Doc.

"I've watched and you've been getting better all along. Wait 'til you get to Cerrillos. The air has something special in it—everyone gets well. Guess it's why there's so much killing; otherwise no one would ever die." Rocky joined in the laughter.

"Maybe I'm going to the wrong place. There may be no need for me there," countered Doc.

"If you can put a broken body back together, there'll be lots of customers," said Rocky. "It's a rough, wild country, and the men who live there are rough and wild, too. Best plan to change your day of rest from Sunday to the middle of the week, though," continued Rocky. "Folks celebrate weekends with guns and liquor."

"Don't scare Doc away," put in Jeb.

"He won't," assured Doc, "I don't expect a garden of Eden."

"That's good, because some folks say it's closer to the other place. I like it—I like the excitement of taming a wild country which someday will belong to the United States. I hope to live to see that," said Jeb. "Cookie, let's start preparing supper now. In about an hour it should be cool enough to reload the animals.

Two hours later the team was heading toward Cerrillos again. As the sun disappeared, so did the heat; before long it was possible to trot the animals. As Jeb and Turning Red had known, the full moon gave plenty of light for Gutsy to lead the mule train.

There were no trees, no hills, except an occasional one of blown sand that would move in the next storm. In this area it was said that the wind blew the sand to the east one day and returned the next day to blow the same sand to the west.

Gutsy looked back over his shoulder and enjoyed the eerie shadows cast by the light from the moon onto the train as it moved forward through the light-colored sand.

The call to circle up came early in the morning. Petre had returned from scouting with the news it was still the same flat, shifting sand ahead, so they should prepare for the heat of the day while the desert still had some coolness.

"We've made about thirty miles, counting the ten we made before our *siesta*," said Jeb. "Let's have some coffee and breakfast after we prepare shelters for our animals and us."

The experience of the long days on the trail helped the men unpack quickly. Gutsy unwrapped another bagful of water. He hauled it from animal to animal, being careful to give each an equal amount. It must last the entire trip across the desert, so he was careful to not spill one precious drop.

"We may have problems ahead," said Flatnose, worried. "Noticed the wind is picking up right smart."

"Isn't that good?" asked a surprised Doc. "I was just thinking we would at least have a breeze."

"Nope, this kind of breeze is the forerunner of a blow; a blow means a sandstorm, even a tornado. A sandstorm can sweep across the whole desert and you're the only thing that ain't blown away. If it's a tornado, you may be blown, too," explained Petre.

"How long does a storm like that generally last?" asked Doc.

"Seen one blow for over a week, counting the buildup and dying down," said Bible John.

"What did you do?" asked Gutsy.

"Prayed a lot, shoveled a lot of sand away from the front of the shelters so the horses, as well as we humans, wouldn't be buried alive," recalled Bible John.

"Ain't time for shoveling, but if you figger you've got a little pull with the Almighty, you could ask for this storm to go north of us," growled Flatnose impatiently.

Jeb and Flatnose decided they could travel at least one more night before the worst of the storm hit. With luck, they'd be past the center of the desert, which meant the wind would have less time to pick up sand.

"If the storm stays in the same direction and we hurry, we just may miss the full fury," said Jeb. "We'll rest only four hours; it'll take another two hours for loading and eating—that means in six hours we should be on our way. If we have no problems we should make it almost to the other side.

The scouts and Flatnose nodded in agreement. Bible John, Doc, Cookie and Gutsy depended on the others to get them through.

"Even if we miss the worst, we're in for some sand," continued Jeb, as he stood face into the rising wind. "When we start again, you'll want to be covered as much as possible. You'll need more than your neckerchiefs. You'll want a scarf that'll cover your entire face.

"Gutsy, in my possible bag you'll find two scarves, one for me and one for a friend—you're that friend. Don't be embarrassed if it's a mite fancy for a teamster—the sand will soon take care of that. When you find them, bring them here so that we have them before we start.

Gutsy hurried to find the scarves. He planned to rest with them at his side.

"Doc, what about you? Look in your saddle bags for a long piece of material that can be wrapped around and around your entire head. I'd also make a suggestion for the next time you travel—you should have a possible bag. Put in it something for every possible emergency. Before this is over we may be needing some of your medical supplies, even may be sorry you gave all that ointment away."

"I do have a possible bag—rather, it's a roll. Each time someone told of a calamity that might happen, I made a note to put a remedy in the roll behind my saddle. You'll be glad to know there is extra ointment and soap in there, too," explained Doc.

"Is my whiskey there?" asked Bible John.

"No," answered Jeb sharply. "When Turning Red gave Gutsy the packhoss, I gave him your cache of whiskey."

"You did what?" gasped Bible John.

"You heard me. We had nothing else he wanted, you know that, and I figgered it would keep them from following us," replied Jeb shortly.

"I was looking forward to that," whimpered Bible John.

"Got whiskey in San Miguel," retorted Jeb. "We'll have to stop there for customs, so you can have a nip or two. 'Til then you need all your wits about you."

"Come and get it, come and get it," called Cookie. "Coffee and wind are both hot."

"Can you make a second pot now," asked Jeb, seeing that Cookie had used only two of the sticks of wood. "Even digging a pit for a fire cain't be done tomorrow. We can refill one of Gutsy's water containers with coffee and tomorrow we'll have tepid coffee, even if we cain't have it boiling hot."

"Better than none," agreed Flatnose. "One good thing about these storms, Injuns hate them just as much as we do."

The food, even with sand added, was good. Everyone joked and pretended this latest problem was a little one—kind people everywhere handled everyday.

"Enjoy these shelters" joked Rocky with a touch of the serious in his voice, "tomorrow it may be blowing so hard we cain't keep them up."

After eating, Cookie fixed lunch packs for several days. No one knew when they might have a fire again. If the storm separated them, Cookie wanted enough food for them to get through several days. Coffee was put into individual water carriers; as well as the large ones from the Comanches. Each man carried his trail cup on his person to save having to stop and unpack whenever they wanted a drink of coffee.

The saddle and pack horses had eye protectors, but for the mules, the men cut small pieces from the soft buffalo hide and laced them to the bridle straps, using the pieces of sinew given them by the Comanches.

NINE

Looks like we can start loading now," announced Jeb, returning from yet another trip outside to look at the sky. "The wind's hot, the sand's hotter. We'll need to wrap all the animals' feet before we load. Foot pads are in the biggest possible sack, Gutsy. Wrap each foot carefully and tie thongs around and around the leg; not too tight. We don't want cooked feet, but we don't want to cut off circulation."

"How many times have these mules made this trip?" asked Doc, getting up from putting pads on the third mule.

"Probably two times, why?" asked Rocky.

"They almost hold their feet out," said Doc, laughing. "I'd say they welcome the pads."

"They do, but mostly it's because the *mulera* has hers on,"answered Petre. "If you can convince the *mulera* to do something, all the rest will hurry to join in."

"Gutsy, start to brush the mules' backs, then shake those saddle blankets good. Sand is like glass and could cut even their tough hides if it gets under their load," ordered Jeb as he looked apprehensively at the sky. "If this storm keeps gathering, we may not stop for a long time. When you put the blankets on, have them hang long to the right side to protect against the blowing sand, and be sure to cinch those packs extry tight. This kind of wind could blow the packs right over, and we don't want to have to stop and reload. Probably Rocky and Petre should help pull on the cinches. This is a tough time for those mules, so let's help them all we can," said Jeb.

For the first time, the mules rebelled. Their rest was short, and the winds were building. Their animal instinct told them to stay protected.

"We may lose our moonlight," said Flatnose, "but I think it will be tomorrow before it's so bad we cain't see the sun or moon."

"We could wait it out here," explained Jeb, "but the closer we get to the other side of the desert the less sand will be in the wind."

"Yep, you're right. If we can make thirty more miles, there's a chance we can locate a dune high enough to protect us," said Flatnose, agreeing with Jeb.

The scouts, Bible John and Cookie nodded. Doc and Gutsy knew nothing of what was ahead. They were glad they were with Jeb, whom they believed knew everything.

"Wrap your faces and necks, now," ordered Jeb. "You'll get used to it, and your skin needs all the protection you can get. Come here, Gutsy, and I'll wrap you. Flatnose, take care of Doc. You other four help each other if you need to. Make sure there is only a slit for your eyes and a small hole to breathe through. Later, you may have to cover the nose completely and breathe through the cloth, but we don't need to do that just yet. If you have gloves, wear them—better to be hot than sandblasted."

"Do you suppose Lucky will recognize me?" asked Gutsy. He laughed.

"That hoss knows what's ahead," guessed Petre. "Lived in Comanche country all his born days. Shouldn't wonder if he couldn't lead us, if we need it."

"Speaking of that," added Jeb, "if any hoss starts to spook, there's a reason. Heard of hoss sense, ain't you? Wal, they have it, and we may need it."

With that, Jeb began his necessary upbraiding of the mules.

"Fall in, fall in, ye misbegotten beasts! If ye think ye got it hard now, wait 'til the whip starts landing. It's worse than this sand. Kick old Bess with both feet. Cookie. Gutsy, yank that lead rope hard. Crack those whips. Make those mules' ears stand up and tremble. Come on now, let's hear that bell jangle.

"Come on, ye goose-rumped goats, let's blaze a trail across this red hot sand that ain't been blazed before. Whooeee! They're getting so anxious to see us racing into Cerrillos they're sending this gawd-awful sand out to greet us. Get up and get going. Forget the sand! Ring that bell! I want to see San Miguel so we can argue with those cheating custom agents. Whoooeee! Crack those whips again and let's go!" shouted Jeb, as he cracked his whip in the air over the heads of the reluctant mules.

Encouraged by their beloved tirade and the sound of the jangling bell, the train started. This time, no shuffling trot could be hear.

Jeb rode up beside Gutsy and Petre, calling, "Keep the pace easy but steady. We may travel all night, so settle in for a long haul."

"Did you ever hear of sleeping in the saddle, Doc?" asked Bible John.

"I've heard of it. Now I suppose you're saying I'll learn to do it," guessed Doc.

"You may, you just may. On the other hand, it may get so exciting we'll all be awake all the time," answered Bible John.

"Tell you what, Bible John, you start your intercessions with the Lawd and add that we all stay awake," taunted Flatnose as he rode on back, checking each load.

There was no danger from renegade Indians, so Flatnose suggested to Gutsy that he ride up and down the train. It would give him something to do. Gutsy agreed. He was struggling to keep the team moving forward.

Flatnose didn't mention he wanted to do this only partly to protect Gutsy, and only partly because he was more experienced with loaded animals in a strong wind storm. He knew it was also because he could not stand to be close to people all the time. Animals, yes, but people at times were too much for him.

Grimly, the train traveled on. They watched the sand-covered sunset, knowing that tomorrow they might not see the sun. They were grateful for the full moon, even though its light was greatly lessened by the blowing sand.

For thirty miles they pushed their way through the swirling, stinging storm. They heard, with fear and dread, the buildup of the wind. They felt, even through all their protection, the sharp bite of the particles as the sand came faster and harder. Their throats were parched; pains gnawed at their bellies. They stretched the animals' endurance to the utmost.

As the moon went down in that darkest period just before the dawn, so did their spirits.

"Dunes ahead! Dunes ahead!" shouted Petre. "We've reached the dunes."

Jeb, Flatnose, Rocky, and Bible John raced ahead to find the perfect spot for protection from the storm, all discouragement and tiredness forgotten. Even the mules sensed the relief and speeded up.

Cookie reached for old Bess's bell to slow them down, when Jeb called, "Over here to the left—we have the spot."

Gutsy came first, guiding Lucky toward the sound of Jeb's voice. He would be glad to get out of his saddle, and if they had to lay over a day, he would be glad for the rest.

"Circle up—circle up," called Jeb.

He helped Gutsy and Cookie lead the team between two huge sand dunes.

"Figured these have been here through a few storms," explained Jeb.

"See that clump of cactus growing there?" asked Petre. "Didn't grow yesterday."

"You may call that prickly bush a cactus, but it looks like a sturdy oak to me," exclaimed Doc, as he dismounted carefully from his hot and sweaty saddle.

"Lean down, Lucky," coaxed Gutsy.

Lucky let Gutsy slid over his head and down to the ground. He tried to stand. *What has happened to my legs*, wondered Gutsy, *they just are not there*. He fell to the ground. Lucky carefully nipped Gutsy's leather shirt and pulled him up, holding him until he could get his land legs.

"You've got yourself a real hoss," exclaimed Rocky.

"Sometimes a man and a hoss are close like that," said Flatnose. "You can be sure that hoss will never let you down."

"Let's put up our shelters against this dune, our backs to the winds. We'd better put the animals in with us, or they may panic and kick up a mess," decided Jeb. "We'll fasten our packs as good as we can, and then tie Gutsy's hides to them. Probably we'll be under sand tomorrow; that will help hold the hides. Bring all our food and all the animals' food inside the shelter first, then the animals."

He was everywhere at once, helping to unload, carrying packs, lacing hides for shelter, encouraging everyone.

"Start thinking, because tonight and tomorrow each one will have a chance to tell his biggest lie, and I plan to out lie you all," shouted Flatnose above the howl of the wind.

"Lookee there. Talk about smart animals. Each one's got his rump turned to the blowing sand, his head lowered just enough so his body protects him. Not one open eye, either," crowed Cookie, as he brought old Bess into the temporary shelter. The other thirty-nine animals followed. The horses had no problems sharing the shelter with either the mules or the humans.

Men and animals waited together for three days, eating, lying, sleeping, and listening to the storm.

Jeb rationed the two-day supply of water and food. There was plenty of smoked buffalo meat, but water would be a grave problem if they were delayed another day.

Burton G. Vose

Lift your eyes to the mountains.

TEN

On the fourth day of the storm, five days after they left the Arkansas River the winds lessened.

Jeb decided it was time to dig out from under the newly blown sand and look around. An entirely new landscape was before them. Their sand dune had grown at least five feet. The path they had walked was gone, the sands were still swirling—some leaving, some staying, evidently content with the new place they had found to settle.

"We'll wait today and tonight," answered Jeb to everyone's unasked question. "We'll spend the time digging out and cleaning the packs. We'll leave early in the morning. If the edge of the desert ain't changed, we have about ten miles to go. We should be through this blistering sand by two in the afternoon. If we are careful with the remaining water, we may make the Cimarron River before our tongues turn black."

"I'll give the animals the last of the grass today," said Cookie.

"And they probably won't believe they have anything," added Petre. "Maybe keep them quiet for a while, though."

"Their stomachs are growling worse than mine," commented Doc cheerfully. He was happy it was time to move on.

"Better pucker up your britches another notch, Doc, or you and they'll part company when you least expect it," suggested Rocky.

"You need to hitch up yours a mite, too," said Flatnose, who had developed a great respect and loyalty for Doc. He was anxious to protect him from any insult.

"When we get to San Miguel, I'm going to have a four-pound steak, preferably without sand on it," announced Bible John, as he hitched his belt up a notch.

"Thought you was craving whiskey," laughed Petre. He wanted the first four-pounder served.

"Whiskey comes later," agreed Bible John. "First I need to pull the back of my belly off the front of my backbone."

"What about Gutsy? He cain't go in a public eating house," said Rocky.

"You're right. My Gawd! He'd be as noticeable as a prostitute in church," agreed Flatnose.

"I've thought a lot about it, but there ain't no way he can avoid going through customs," said Jeb.

"Why do I have to be afraid out here?" asked Gutsy in a surprised voice. "I thought my worries were back in Westport."

"Old Barnes may have a notice out about you. Mebbe sent it over the country by mail express. That is, if there was an express coming this way," answered Flatnose.

"Well, if it costs much money, he wouldn't bother with that. After all, he's got Herman right there," exclaimed Gutsy.

Let's look at it this way," said Doc. "There's probably no cause to worry even if there's been an express—the description would be for a blonde boy. If Gutsy waits to take his bath until we are through San Miguel, no one would suspect him. His skin is almost Indian Brown by now, and he's riding a Comanche horse that acts as if they have always been together. We can act as if he is Comanche boy who guides the team and helps Cookie."

"Gol dang, Doc, you're right! Nobody'd recognize him, not even old Barnes hisself! Why, he even has a new name," exclaimed Flatnose. "But, just for extry measure, I'll have my gun primed."

"That's okay, Flatnose, you can pretend you're keeping me from running away," said Gutsy. His laugh was a little wry.

Even before the false dawn, the entire camp was humming. The horses were saddled and waiting. The packs, dug out the night before, needed only a brushing as they were lined up for the waiting mules.

Gutsy sang as he dropped the shaken-out saddle pads over the mules' backs. He remembered to let the right side (the wind side) hang a little longer to protect the animals' bodies from the sharp, pointed sand grains. He worked slowly, staying just ahead of the packers to prevent more sand blowing under the packs.

Cookie gave each man a cup of water before giving the rest to the loaded mules and saddled horses.

"Hardly enough to wet their tongues," announced Cookie.

"They'll be hard to handle as we get close to the Cimarron. We'll all have to step sharply and hold them back as long as we can, or they'll founder," said Jeb. "I hope there's a small stream where we can let them have water before we get to the Cimarron where they'll want to swim before we can unload them."

"Now, let's start."

"Come on, you misbegotten sons of this howling sandstorm. You wallowing bundles of misery. You goose-rumped goats. You sons of Satan! Let's get these next miserable ten miles behind us. Cookie! Kick old Bess and slap her on her rump. Shake the sand out of her bell and let it jangle. Gutsy! Jerk that rope and lead them out. Step it up! If you want to feel the cool soothing water of the Cimarron, get up and go! Begone! Begone, I say! Let's find those water-bogged trees and kiss this burning hell good-bye," called Jeb.

Still wearing blinders and still fighting the pelting sand, the team moved forward at their usual plodding pace for the first five miles. They grunted and strained to show their distress until their sensitive noses began to smell water. At the first whiff, they reared their heads, they brayed the news, their eyes brightened, their steps quickened—even without the bell—and the battle for control was on.

Jeb placed the riders and horses, even the pack horse, in front the hurrying team. Jeb took Gutsy's place as lead man and held back on old Bess. Gutsy joined the men in front of the team as they paced their horses. Cookie rang the bell loudly, but slowly. The mules were frustrated between their desire to be obedient to the bell and their animal knowledge that water was straight ahead.

For the first four miles the discipline held; but as they reached the last mile, even the horses began whinnying for the water. Flatnose and the scouts knew it would be impossible to block the train with the horses any longer. The mules would simply stampede around the horses. Therefore, the men fell back along the train to lasso some of the most rambunctious and hold them back by pulling on the lassos.

Flatnose lassoed one and turned it over to Gutsy; about six mules further back he lassoed one for himself. Bible John tried to show his skill with the rope. After a second throw, he did lasso one and held on. Each scout also chose a mule to lasso and hold back. In this manner, the team reached a small freshet feeding off the larger river. This was what Jeb had hoped for, a shallow stream too small for them to roll and destroy the packs.

After the animals and men had had enough water, with their cargo still dry, the team moved forward to the Cimarron. They crossed this most welcome landmark to the grove of trees where Jeb planned to make camp.

Gutsy reined Lucky to a sliding stop near a big tree, threw the reins over Lucky's head; and as he was trained, Lucky lowered his head for Gutsy to slide down. This time, as he landed, Gutsy sank deep into a hole. Lucky tried to lift him up, but the hole would not give Gutsy up. Gutsy tried to climb out, but each time he moved his foot, something under it slipped and slid, giving him no footing. He fell face down in the grass. Lucky whinnied, as if for help, before he grabbed Gutsy's shirt to pull. Doc, close by, heard the crashing and whinnying and rushed to help. Gutsy had already turned, and taken hold of Lucky's bridle. Lucky stepped back and pulled Gutsy from the hole.

The others came and joined Doc and Gutsy, who were staring in open-mouthed astonishment at the top of Gutsy's worn and dirty moccasins.

"Gawd Almighty! That's money!" whispered Petre.

"Where you get that?" asked Jeb.

"There—from that hole—where I fell," answered the stunned Gutsy.

"Betcha there's more," exclaimed Flatnose. "Why, Gutsy, you could be rich!"

Jeb reached down and felt in the hole.

"Yes," he said. "Cookie, bring a pan. Better make it a large one, this hole is deep. Here, Gutsy, hold out your hand and see what it feels like to be loaded with money," said Jeb. He laughed at his own joke.

Time after time, Jeb dug into the hole and brought out coins. Gutsy's eyes grew bigger and bigger. For the third time this trip his mouth opened and closed, but the words did not come. Lucky stuck his head over Gutsy's shoulder to nuzzle him, but all Gutsy could do was rub his head against Lucky's. One reason—his hands were full of money.

Cookie returned with a pan, jabbering, "Ain't he the luckiest kid? Now ain't he? Started this trip without nothing but the clothes on his back. Now he's rich. Glad for him, but I could use one little fistful of his luck."

Jeb emptied the hole, gave the pan full of money to Gutsy and suggested, "Each of you should stomp around the area. No doubt some traveler ran into problems and buried his money. If there was more than one in the party, probably will be other caches."

"Tell you what—I'm hungry! If Cookie will start some food, I'll stomp and share anything I might find with him," said Doc.

"Better yet, let's all share whatever we find," said Bible John.

"I'll share this gladly," agreed Gutsy.

"Naw, this pact goes for new finds," said Flatnose. "First you pay your contract."

"Okay, but I'll help Cookie. I couldn't possibly need more than this," said Gutsy.

He carried his heavy pan of coins to the spot where Cookie was unloading, preparing to make supper.

It was the smell of fresh coffee that stopped the stomping and digging.

"Appears like only one poor bugger was here," said Flatnose, eagerly holding out his hastily wiped-out trail mug.

"Hope he made it to help," said Gutsy as he poured coffee into the mugs of the team members.

"After two days of stale desert heated coffee and three days of none, this tastes like pure ambrosia," said Doc, complimenting Cookie.

"Never did taste ambrosia," declared Flatnose, "but even if it's real good, this has got to be better."

"Between boiling coffee and fresh baked biscuits, this place must rank higher than the Garden of Eden when it come to smells," said Bible John, as he sniffed the delightful odor and sipped the delicious brew.

"Since someone might say we have just been through hell, we might be closer to that garden then we know," said Jeb. "I'm grateful to have the crossing behind us. The worst is over. We still have to go through customs and somehow protect Gutsy and now his money. But, with all of us together, we should have brains enough to come up with a plan."

"How much money did you find?" asked Petre.

"Don't know," mumbled Gutsy through a big mouthful of hot biscuit.

"You don't know? Why not? Didn't you count it?" asked Rocky.

"Can't. Never saw this kind of money before," replied Gutsy, spreading out a handful for all to see. "You can see, it isn't dollars," said Gutsy.

"Ain't pesos," said Petre.

"Ain't doubloons," announced Rocky, turning the coins over and over.

"Ain't piasters," added Cookie.

"Ain't guineas," said Jeb.

"Doc, ain't these crowns and that there one a shilling? asked Flatnose.

"They might well be, but very old ones. However, no matter how old, they are still money," agreed Doc. "But what would a man with English money be doing in this area?"

"No darned good, you can betcha," snarled Flatnose, rubbing his nose, remembering the way he'd received it at the hands of an angry Englishman. "Anyhow, it's Gutsy's now, and I'll personally finish the man that tries to take it away from him."

"A small fortune, I believe," answered Doc. "Since this is actually Mexico, it was probably meant to buy trouble for the United States. We're rivals of the English, remember."

"Will it buy my contract?" asked Gutsy.

"Yes, and pay for schooling and start you in business," said Doc, after figuring the amount of money at the current prices.

"Then after my contract is paid, we'll divide it evenly," announced Gutsy. "I'll worry about school and work later."

"I don't want none of it," said Rocky. "As far as I'm concerned, wouldn't do me any good."

"The money's yours," said Flatnose.

"Keep it, kid. Got me the best job in the world and all the money I can use. If'n I had too much, I'd probably get lazy and fat and die of heart problems."

"It's a gift from the Lord. He gave it to you and therefore you must keep it," pronounced Bible John in his best pontifical manner. He squared his shoulders as he clamped his jaws shut to show to all the matter was now settled.

"Is there a bank in Cerrillos?" asked Doc.

If not, soon will be with all the gold and gold hunters there," said Jeb. "We'll find a safe place for it, if we can just get past the greedy eyes in San Miguel."

"I have a proposal. When we get to San Miguel, Gutsy can buy us the best feed in town," said Doc. "I'll pay for it at first, because we can't show this old money—especially since it's owned by our Indian slave boy."

"Get out your biggest coins," said Flatnose. "I've got a frightful longing for fresh food."

"Gutsy will even buy you a little of the finest whiskey they have," said Doc.

"A little, but not too much. We've got to protect our train, our slave boy, and his fortune," cautioned Jeb.

"Whooppee! I can taste that juicy steak now," howled Cookie. "One I don't cook myself, although I haven't found anyone yet who can beat my cooking. Even if I do have to say so myself."

"We all agree, you're the best, but we could stand a fresh vegetable," said Jeb.

"You're right, Jeb, about just a little whiskey, I mean," agreed Bible John. "Don't need any loose-lipping and wild stories about buried treasures."

"Thank you, Bible John, but when we get to Cerrillos you are on your own. Guess we'd best think of our animals," said Jeb ruefully, "We had so much excitement we've forgotten to unload."

Everyone fell to, and the tired, patient animals were unloaded; their packs were lined up for the morning march, and the animals were allowed to graze and sleep as they wished.

Later in the evening, over another cup of Cookie's trail coffee, Jeb said, "Before we go any father we've got to prepare for customs. For the regular goods, we have a letter from the Mexican mine owner, signed by the Mexican governor, ordering these things. Therefore, on a regular basis customs ain't no problem. But, we have two extry things to worry about. Doc's money and Gutsy's. The customs will expect Doc to have a bankroll; they will try to tax as much as they can, but we can get most of it by."

"Is there anything I can do that will help?" asked Doc.

They should be so glad to have a Doc, they should pay you," growled Flatnose.

"I'm thinking," said Jeb. "Gutsy need the most protection. The Spanish king claims a royal fifth of every treasure found. I'm not willing for Gutsy to pay this. First of all, it's not ore, but coins. They are not Spanish, but English. I feel the same way about Doc's money—it's his'n."

"I'd hate to pay a fifth," agreed Doc.

"Yours might even be more, 'cause you're American," grunted Flatnose.

"Here's a plan that may work. However, if it doesn't in this land of bribery no one will even be mad if we try and fail," said Jeb. "We'll cut the two dressed buffalo hides into strips and lay the coins flat on the strips. Then we'll double over the sides and ends, making a long strip. We'll soak the hides in water so they shrink. Next, we'll drape these over the hosses, in front and behind the saddles like decorations. May be too many for the hosses. We may have to use a mule or two. With our mouths sealed, we'll all ride into San Miguel with special decorations on our hosses."

"Hey, what a plan," said Petrc. "The customs people kin inspect everything, but we'll ride out with Gutsy and Doc as rich as they are now."

"Isn't it too early to make the strips?" asked Rocky.

"No," answered Jeb. "We want them to be sweaty and old looking when we ride in for inspection."

"Now for sure, we will have to guard the train," said Rocky.

"Your Indian slave boy will be there," said Gutsy as he laughed.

"So will old Mike and me," said Flatnose, patting his gun lovingly. "When you order that fancy dinner Gutsy's buying, just have two brought out to the team."

"Why not have all of them outside?" asked Doc.

"That'd make them suspicious. They'll be expecting news and trail stories," said Jeb.

"Okay, you give them the stories, and the rest'll mosey in and out, all the time keeping a weather eye on our team." Flatnose chuckled as he thought of the game ahead.

"Don't forget, you have to guard the Indian boy," said Gutsy. They all laughed together.

"Ain't no real lie," said Flatnose. "After all, you're a Comanche."

"Let's cut the buffalo hide and start it soaking," said Cookie. "Hate to see all that coin laying about when we don't have Gutsy's new family to protect us."

"Look at that boy cut," said Jeb. "Your work as a saddler sure made you a fast man with the knife."

"Glad I can do something right. You know, it's funny. Now I don't have to work for old Barnes, I like leather," Gutsy said, laughing.

"About old Barnes—don't rest easy," said Flatnose. "We've still got a long way to go, and lots of people would like these coins. We're in Mexico now, and it's a wild country. This far from Mexico City ain't no law but the six-shooter."

"But if we hide the money. . . ," began Gutsy.

"Other man hid the money, and he still didn't keep it, did he? cautioned Flatnose. "Here we can expect Injuns, bandits, military thieves, or all three. Sure we got a right to be here—Jeb's got a letter—but, if you have to go to Mexico City to prove it, your goods are left behind, with no one to protect them."

"That isn't good, is it?" said Gutsy.

"But we're going to play it smart and not let anything like that happen," said Flatnose.

"Here," said Cookie, "two new decorations are ready."

"Put them in the stream to soak overnight, and in the morning we'll put them over the hosses to dry and shape," said Jeb.

"Mebbe before we get there we can even put a tassel on the ends," suggested Petre. "Gutsy can cut fringe or something."

"Good idea. We'll save that for tomorrow, after we make camp," agreed Jeb.

Just before the campfire became the only available light, Jeb announced, "We've got seventeen strips, two for each hoss and one for old Bess. Doc is still carrying some money, but that would be expected. I believe we can get through to Cerrillos without losing much."

Flatnose nodded in agreement.

"Tomorrow we start nine days more of travel before we reach the first settlement, San Miguel," Jeb continued. "We'll see the Sangre de Cristos in just a couple of days, but we travel through the passes, not over the mountains, a longer but somewhat easier route. Tomorrow, after the team is underway, Flatnose and I will try to find fresh meat."

"I shoot very well," said Bible John.

"I'm depending on that, 'cause from now on I want four armed guards around the train at all times," answered Jeb to Bible Johns unasked request to go hunting.

"What if you two have problems?" asked Rocky.

"Good thing you asked. Each of us, excepting Gutsy, has at least one six-shooter. If you hear five rapid shots, circle up the team and prepare to fight. If you hear four rapid shots, two of you come to help us, but never leave the team completely unguarded," ordered Jeb. "And if we hear the same from you, we'll come running, wherever we may be."

"I'll be wearing my guns from now on," stated Cookie.

"Tonight we start two people on each watch; Rocky and Gutsy will take the first watch; Petre and Bible John, the second. Flatnose and I will take the dawn watch," said Jeb.

"I believe I could stand watch from now on," offered Doc.

"Thank you, Doc. I'll give you and Cookie the hardest job and the most important tonight. Keep the fire going, make sure there's hot coffee for the men on watch, and guard that leather we've got soaking in the stream. After tonight you and Gutsy can switch back and forth. One stand watch and one guard the camp.

"If you should happen to see smoke signals, call me," said Flatnose. "I might be able to read them."

"Let's saddle up, Gutsy! Wait, I'll saddle both hosses, and you better get me a trail mug of coffee and see if you can find a couple of leftover biscuits," said Rocky. "I know we're a mite early, but you need some training."

Sandstone and piñons *Rhea Coleman*

ELEVEN

"There they be," shouted Petre, pointing toward the far right horizon. "Those be the Sangre de Cristos! Whenever I get close, I want to sing."

"Who's the poet now?" asked Gutsy, teasing.

"Just you wait, every man finds his spot on this earth, and when he does, his whole being knows it," said Petre. "When I got to America with my parents I knew it was my country, even as a child; now I know this is the part of my country especially for me."

"See what you mean. I think I'll choose this one, too," said Gutsy, drinking in the wide-open spaces; the blue, blue sky with the white-topped beauty of the Sangre de Cristos edging the vista.

"Perhaps you will," agreed Petre. "But when you really find your spot, ain't choosing you'll do, you'll just know—like Flatnose and the prairie. Some might say it's because you're older, but ain't so—a man just knows."

"Petre, are those signal fires?" asked Gutsy as he pointed to the left, away from the mountains.

"Call Flatnose," urged Petre. "He says he sometimes can read them."

"Flatnose! Flatnose! I think we have a signal fire to the left," called Gutsy, riding Lucky back to the train.

"Yep, says a big group of animals are moving toward the mountains," read Flatnose.

"What else?" demanded Petre.

"Cain't tell. You know, it's all symbols—so many long puffs mean something, so many short puffs something else, and interrupted puffs something else. All I can make out is moving animals. Could be us. Could be antelopes. Could be any kind of animals. Probably not buffalo, though. That's a long, big puff with a small one riding on top like a hump. Leastwise, that's what a brave told me."

"Anyway, we know there are at least two groups of Injuns," said Petre.

"Two?" echoed Gutsy.

"Yep. If one is talking, at least one more should be reading," Petre said.

"Gives me shivers, knowing how Injuns love mule stew," muttered Cookie.

"Now that signal means pass," exclaimed Flatnose. "But I cain't tell if it says let them pass or don't."

"But it does make it pretty sure they're talking about us, doesn't it?" asked Gutsy. He wasn't sure which way was good and which was bad.

"Could be, but we've traveled seven days, and they've been around us all the time; never once caused us any problems," reasoned Flatnose.

"I wish Turning Red was here. He'd help us," exclaimed Gutsy.

"We have only two more days to travel," comforted Doc. "We've come a long way."

Five rapid shots rang out.

"Circle up! Circle up! called Petre, even though Cookie and Gutsy were already starting the circle. "Circle up! Make it tight and be prepared to fight."

Within twenty minutes, the animals were circled, still carrying their packs, marching slowly around and around the circle.

Jeb and Bible John reached them just as they were trying to decide whether to unload and prepare to camp, or just keep marching.

"Military detachment, maybe thirty-forty men coming," yelled Jeb as he and Bible John brought their racing horses to rump-down stops. "It's too early to camp, so let's proceed as usual, except all of us will be close to the train, guns ready."

Gutsy mounted Lucky, jumping high and grabbing on. He led the team out in a straight line again.

"Remember, Gutsy, you don't talk! Don't say a word. Grunt if you have to, but not one word. If they speak to you, act like you don't understand. Look alive, and let's get on," ordered Jeb.

Slowly the train started forward. The six armed men rode along the sides—three to the right and three to the left. As the detachment drew near, Jeb rode out to meet them. Because Jeb rode alone, El Capitan also rode alone. Both men met at about the center of the distance between the two.

The train kept moving slowly forward.

Jeb greeted the El Capitan and explained in his, at best, poor Spanish that they were returning to Santa Fe, bringing tools and necessities for the Ortiz Gold Mine.

El Capitan just glared.

Jeb continued in his poor Spanish that he had papers of authority from the governor at Santa Fe.

Still no answer from El Capitan.

"We are on our way to San Miguel to present ourselves and our papers to the customs officer," added Jeb.

Show me your papers," ordered El Capitan.

"They are in my saddle bag. Follow me," answered Jeb, turning Crown toward the train.

El Capitan followed. He looked the papers over carefully, turning each page and scowling.

No one breathed.

Jeb saw one page was upside down, yet the capitan scowled at it in exactly the same manner. Jeb realized El Capitan could not read.

"El Capitan, right here these papers say your government will protect us," said Jeb, pointing to a paragraph on the third page. "See, it says because of the needs of the Ortiz Gold Mine, this mule team is protected."

El Capitan squinted closer.

Jeb retraced each word, pretending to allow the capitan time to read.

El Capitan raised his head, drew back his shoulders, and said, "We must obey our governor. We will escort you to the mines." He squinted once more at the unfathomable paragraph. "Let us start immediately. Your mules are already moving on."

"As you say, Capitan. Cookie, keep the team moving, stretch out! Stretch out!" called Jeb.

No one questioned, or even looked back, the train of mules continued forward and when they reached the military detachment the soldiers rode on each side.

"We'll reach San Miguel tomorrow," whispered Jeb in English. "Maybe they'll leave us then."

Camp was larger that night. Cookie and his helper Gutsy prepared more biscuits and coffee than they had served when Turning Red and his followers had been with them. Both groups shared guard duty, side by side.

Early morning found Doc and Gutsy both helping Cookie. Evidently the military detachment hadn't been as well supplied as the mule train and they showed their delight in the sourdough biscuits and the coffee by eating their fill—and their fill was fantastic.

Next morning found the team members eager to be loaded and on their way. It was safer to travel in numbers, but the military and the Indians were bitter enemies and the team felt it would have been better to be alone on the plain.

"Like I said, we'll reach San Miguel tomorrow," whispered Jeb in English. "Maybe they'll leave us then."

"Don't do anything to upset them, we may need their help with customs," cautioned Jeb.

Right on schedule, the next afternoon, just at *siesta* time, the mule team and its military escort arrived in San Miguel. Even though it was a small village with only nine mud (adobe) houses and three corrals, it was wonderful to see.

Jeb and El Capitan went immediately to the customs officer where Jeb presented his papers.

El Capitan was confident he understood both his duty and his rank, therefore he ordered the customs men to: "Make all haste—these men are bringing goods ordered by the governor."

Jeb smiled at El Capitan and asked, "Would you honor us by sharing a feast of celebration, your troops, too? Our cook and the slave boy will stay with the mules, but the rest of us would enjoy food and good whiskey. That is, we would if it's all right with you and the customs officers."

"Do you have twenty dollars to pay for it?" asked the surprised and pleased capitan.

"The doctor is so grateful for your escort he wants to express his thanks by paying for the party. You know, he plans to set up practice in Cerrillos and thinks you might put in a good word for him," said Jeb and winked his eye to show them both he'd just shared a great secret."

"Well, if he wants to pay, why not?" exclaimed El Capitan. He winked back.

"In that case, I'll ask him for forty dollars and maybe you'll have a little left for the party to continue on tomorrow after we strike out for Santa Fe," urged Jeb as he planted the idea they would not need an escort the rest of the way.

"That's an even better idea. Say, I'd better help my friend here with your things. He doesn't read too good, so I'll just read the same paragraph you read to me and have him order the party," said El Capitan.

"If you like, why not invite your friend to the party?" encouraged Jeb. "You talk with him, get the party set up, and I'll go get the money from Doc. I'll tell the rest so they can be prepared for a real celebration."

"Si, si, Senor. You do that!" shouted El Capitan, slapping Jeb on the back in anticipation of the party.

"Oh, I just had another thought. Would it be all right if we camp about a mile down the road? We've been traveling a long time, and we'd like to bathe in the stream. It would keep the animal smells away from our party, too," asked Jeb.

"Si, si, mi amigo," said the customs agent, while El Capitan nodded agreement.

Quickly Jeb explained to the anxious men what he had accomplished.

Doc said, "Let's make it a sixty-dollar party. That should keep them out of our way until we're settled in Cerrillos. After all, Gutsy can afford it."

"Bible John, we know you have a powerful thirst, but, if you wish to continue with us, you'd better be able to travel out of here at about three o'clock tomorrow morning," threatened Jeb.

"Actually, I think I'd rather wait to celebrate when we get to Cerrillos," answered Bible John. "We have so much going on, I don't want to miss any of it. This has certainly been the most interesting trip I've ever made."

"In that case, you could put a small bottle in your saddle bag. I'm not going to check this last day of travel," said Jeb.

"Last day? Will we get to Cerrillos tomorrow?" asked Gutsy.

"Think so. We don't need to go to Santa Fe since all our goods go to Cerrillos. We can save a lot of time and disappointed people," answered Jeb.

"Whoopee, then I can get a job," exclaimed Gutsy. He wasn't used to being a treasurer finder as yet.

"Hush! Don't speak another word, Gutsy," warned Flatnose. "We've got to get there first. Remember, you're a slave boy."

"You're right," agreed Gutsy.

"We'll take turns going to the party. Whenever you're there, make lots of jokes, talk to everyone, eat a lot, and encourage everyone to eat and drink. Then slip out and stand guard while others go and do the same. After we're sure they won't notice, we'll leave. That's when I'll give this extry twenty dollars to El Capitan so the party can continue," said Jeb.

"We'll plan to start loading the mules about one thirty; we should be high-tailing it by three," he continued. "Sorry, Gutsy, you can't go to the party you're paying for, but there's lots of parties ahead. Anyway, we'll see you get lots of the food."

"Doc, Petre, and Flatnose, you go first. Have a good time, but stay alert. I'll be in and out, trying to keep El Capitan and the customs officers in a jovial mood. Tell them good stories and see to it that everybody is happy. Remember, if you run out of windies make some up!"

Ortiz Mountains *Rhea Coleman*

TWELVE

Long before the first inquiring fingers of the sun wiggled over the eastern horizon, anyone looking could have seen a long line of mules winding its way through the pass, heading for Cerrillos.

During the late hours of the party, Petre and Rocky staged a contest between the military and the civilian men, proving once and for all which would make the best mule skinners. Determined to show that the army could out-shout, out-swear, and out-whip any red-necked civilians, all caution was set aside and Jeb was able to start the team without the least chance of being heard. It took Petre and Rocky two hours to catch up with the team, because the contest was so popular, and the men so determined.

"Those fellows enjoyed themselves so much we couldn't get away," said Rocky.

"One or two of them could give even you lessons," added Petre. "Guess the army puts a little added flavor in their tongues."

"Looks like Santa Fe is coming to life," commented Flatnose as he saw some lights to the far right.

"Ain't this country amazing?" exclaimed Jeb. "Santa Fe must be at least ten miles to our right."

"What is the white on top of the mountains?" asked Gutsy.

"Let's see, this is June third, so that may well be snow," answered Jeb. "Probably cain't see it now, but over a group of the Sangre de Cristos, the snow, because of the shapes of the mountains, looks like a huge thunderbird in flight. Some people live their lives according to it. They plant their crops when the thunderbird is gone. They go to camps when it returns to the tops of the mountains, they plan their hunts and even their wars are guided by it."

"Do you believe it?" asked Gutsy. Ready to learn the legend and live by it if Jeb did.

"No, but I never question one who does. These people are usually wise. They've lived a long time, following their own way, so

I respect it. If one of the wise ones gave me advice based on it, I'd follow it," answered Jeb.

"If you ever have a chance to learn these legends, be sure you do," added Flatnose. "This country has been here a long time, and if you want to live here you must recognize its past is as important to remember as its future."

"Jeb, what's going to happen now?" asked Gutsy, almost dreading the end of the journey. He had no idea of his next step, nor how to take it.

First of all, we still don't know if you've been posted or not. So you'd best wait outside Cerrillos until we get information," said Jeb.

"Yeah, like Flatnose said, I would be as conspicuous as a painted lady in church," acknowledged Gutsy. "How long will I have to wait?"

"Cain't say. As soon as we get to Cerrillos, Rocky, Petre, Doc, and Bible John will be free. They can walk around and look for posters. Petre knows the sheriff, so he can mosey over there. It's natural for Doc to get a room in a good hotel, so he can look there. Cain't be sure Bible John will return; but he will head to one of the bars and he can ask there. Rocky will try to find out what he can; then he can hunt up Bible John to find out what he knows," explained Jeb.

"That may take all afternoon," figured Gutsy.

"Mebbe longer. If it gets too long, we'll all camp out with you, or else Doc will get you into the hotel. We should have it all fixed up, the money put safely away and your name cleared by tomorrow noon, at the very latest," explained Jeb.

Gutsy sighed, partly in disappointment and partly in fear of the unknown future.

"We've passed into the area now. Two miles to the right is the town and off to the left a couple more miles is one of the most active mines. However, we'll go to the mine office in town. We'll carry our decorations inside and ask for them to be safely stored," continued Jeb.

"These hogbacks you see are the beginning of the Ortiz mountain range. See, they have natural caves that make good hideaways. You can easily hide out here," said Rocky. "Thought I'd go on into town, sign out on the job, collect my pay, find any news I can and ride back here. If you run into trouble, here's one of my six-shooters. Fire it in the air five times, and I'll hurry even faster."

"I'll try to have you in a good bed by tonight, Gutsy," promised Doc. "I don't speak Spanish as easily as the others, but I do well enough to find out if there's been an express. I'll act as if I'm expecting a letter and ask about any mail from Westport. Be sure if there's trouble I'll be here as soon as I can."

"There's a lot of English spoken here, Doc. Look sharp and so must you, Gutsy," said Jeb as they rode on.

Gutsy led his beloved roan around a steep uprising of hogback rocks, through a narrow opening between two slanting slabs of red stone. As Rocky had suggested, he hid in a natural cave big enough for Lucky to be with him.

"Hey, you and these hogbacks are almost the same color," whispered Gutsy. He sat down to wait—and wait.

It seemed only seconds later when Lucky nudged Gutsy, who woke with a start. He looked around, trying to remember where he was and why. Again Lucky nudged him. Gutsy started to look around, but halted mid-turn. He gasped. There, in full daylight, was a stopped team and wagon. He saw two men with their hands high above their heads, and another man with a gun, motioning toward something in the wagon.

"Lucky, I can't even aim this thing," whispered Gutsy, picking up the six-shooter.

The shorter of the two men gave the masked man with the gun a very heavy bag. The masked man motioned them back into the wagon. He fired his guns at them. This caused the team to run away with the wagon that carried the two panicked men who were possibly gun shot.

Gutsy watched. He tried, but he could not move. He was scared. He watched as the bandit stopped firing at the wagon. He watched as the bandit moved closer to his cave. He watched as the bandit dug into the gravelly red earth. He watched as the bandit buried the sack and covered it with small and large stones. He watched the robber throw away his handkerchief mask. He watched as the man rode away in the direction of Santa Fe.

Gutsy realized he did not know the men in the wagon. He did not know the bandit, nor did he know what was in the bag. He only knew where it was buried.

Gutsy and Lucky went to the spot. Gutsy dug up the bag which was so heavy Lucky had to kneel down and let Gutsy drag it onto his back. Gutsy climbed on Lucky's back and together they went in search of Jeb.

As Gutsy entered Cerrillos, he remembered the six-shooter. He raised it above his head and pulled the trigger. He pulled it once, twice, three times, four times and five!

The streets of Cerrillos emptied. People hid under boards, behind animal packs, indoors, and behind trees. Hearing the signal, Jeb, Flatnose, Bible John, Doc, Rocky, Petre and Cookie came running.

What in God's name are you doing here?" shouted Jeb, as he ran toward Gutsy, who was riding tall in his saddle, holding the bag in front of him.

"In the name of the Lord, put down that gun," yelled Bible John. "Be careful doing it—there's still one more shot."

"What is it, Gutsy?" asked Doc, as he ran to the side of Lucky and lifted Gutsy down.

"Don't know, but a man with a cloth covering most of his face shot at a wagon with two men and this sack in it. The men gave the masked man the sack. He fired at them and their horses. The horses ran away with the wagon and the men. The bandit buried the sack and left. I dug up the sack and hightailed it here," gasped Gutsy. "I didn't know where anyone was, so I did as Rocky said and fired the gun five times."

"What's he saying?" asked an onlooker. "Where are the men he wants? asked another. "What did he do?" asked a latecomer. Questions were everywhere, but no one waited for an answer.

Jeb stepped forward, took the bag down, and called for the mine owner.

"Cliff, didn't you send a gold shipment out to Santa Fe?" asked Jeb as soon as the owner came to the group.

"Two men should have just left, maybe half an hour or an hour ago," replied Cliff.

"Well probably this is your gold. Best get two posses, one to find your wagon and men and one to hunt the bandit," drawled Jeb.

"Who's this kid?" asked the sheriff, just arriving.

"He's my ward," answered Doc. "Don't spend time worrying about him. You'd better get your posses and chase the thief before he gets away or your men get killed."

"Doc, you take Gutsy to the hotel," said Jeb. "We'll meet later."

"I'll stable his horse as I get ours," said Rocky.

"Can't I go with one of the posses?" asked Gutsy.

Doc shook his head and took him to the hotel.

Gutsy looked around. It was the grandest thing he had ever seen. Four tall posts supported a soft bed covered by a gorgeous red velvet coverlet. There were two chairs, so soft he felt he was sinking when he sat down. There was a marble-topped table and a huge white pitcher with red flowers painted on it. There was a big white bowl under the magnificent pitcher. At the windows were long red velvet drapes. One wall opened to a special place to hang extra clothes.

Sure, Gutsy thought, *people who lived in a place like this would have lots of clothes. Why, maybe a different outfit for each day.*

Gutsy had time, so he looked again at each thing. He needed to get used to this grandeur before Doc returned. Gutsy knew Doc planned to replace the leather clothes he had worn for two and a half months. He tried to imagine how it would feel to wear anything else. He looked down at his worn and mended moccasins. Perhaps Doc would buy new ones.

Nothing about his life on the frontier or as a bonds boy to old Barnes had prepared him for this. Why, this grand room was for just himself. It was hard to believe, but Doc's room was even grander.

He was still thinking and testing when Doc returned with two men and many boxes. The two men brought a huge metal tub (on a set of wheels) buckets of hot and cold water, soap and towels.

"This is really a bathtub," explained Doc. "It's shaped differently from those in Westport, so I'm not surprised you didn't recognize it." He winked at Gutsy. "The men will fill the tub, and you can bathe yourself. When you're ready, one of the men will rinse you off. Don't worry if you don't get all the soap out of your hair. We'll go to the barber and have him wash it when he cuts it."

Doc started to unpack the new clothes. A red flannel shirt, a pair of ready-made pants, two huge handkerchiefs—one to wear around the throat and one for his pocket. There was a pair of long johns to wear under the pants and a new pair of Indian-made moccasins.

"Need these things here, I understand, so I bought them," said Doc, holding up the summer weight long johns.

Doc waited to see if Gutsy knew how to bathe indoors. When he was satisfied everything was all right, he picked up the leather britches and shirt.

"All they're good for is to be burned," Doc said.

Gutsy was not too anxious to have help from strange men, but if they came with the room, he decided he would play along. Besides, he had never worn long johns nor regular pants. He might need their assistance.

After the transformation, Gutsy and Doc went outside. They met a returning posse driving the wagon, damaged, but still able to roll. Parts were missing, lost forever during its wild, twisting, crazy race over the rocks, down into the arroyos, and back up over the hills. Both Ben and Joe were dazed and bruised. Ben was badly wounded in the left shoulder. Both were scared and grateful the pose had found them.

The pair told of the masked holdup man. They explained that he had come at them suddenly from somewhere out of the caves in the rough country. They admitted they were so busy trying to stop the runaway team they did not know which direction he went.

Doc cleaned the wounds and told them the rest of the story. They were relieved to know the gold was safe and another posse was still hunting the bandit.

"Imagine that," said Ben. "Where's the kid? I still have a right arm, and I want to shake his hand."

"This is our Gutsy," said Doc, bringing Gutsy where everyone could see him.

"Gol darn! He's just a kid" exclaimed the wounded man. "Never seen him before. Where'd he come from?"

"He came with mule train from Westport; he's my ward. He's the blood brother of Turning Red, the Comanche. He's your helper and should be your friend," proclaimed Doc in a stern voice.

"He's got my hand," said Ben.

"And mine," said Joe. "The mine should show its appreciation, too."

"Maybe they'll give me a job," said Gutsy.

"Probably will, but you ought to grow a mite first," said Ben kindly.

"I'm fourteen, and I can work hard," stated Gutsy.

"Wait, Gutsy. All in good time," said Doc. "Remember you have some unfinished business that has to be dealt with."

"But Doc, I want to stay here. I know this is where I want to live. There's something in the air. I know it's the place for me," said Gutsy.

Doc patted Gutsy's shoulder.

"Look, Doc. You're going to set up practice and you'll need a house, and I can help you in that. Maybe you'd let me make a trip or so with Jeb, and...and you could teach me to be a Doc. Will you think about it, Doc" I can be real handy," urged Gutsy.

"I'd like to have you live with me as a son, Gutsy. I'll be glad to teach you when I can, but first things first. Your legal status must be cleared up," said Doc.

"What legal status?" snorted Joe. "No questions asked here. Almost everyone I know has an unclear legal status. We are runaways, criminals, adventurers, hoodlums, army deserters, ex-everythings. We're a bunch of social misfits that have found our place, so why should he have to worry about his status?"

"If I don't, my younger brother will have to work for a real mean man. That's why I want to pay off my contract; but I still want to live here," explained Gutsy.

"That's different, but if you're really worried, why not get your brother here, too," suggested Ben.

Maybe I can," grinned Gutsy, "after I pay old Barnes. Here comes the other posse. Let's see if they got the bandit."

"Would you know him?" asked Joe.

"No, he was still wearing the mask when he rode away, so I never saw his face," said Gutsy.

The other posse, including Gutsy's teammates, rode by, turned their horses over to the stable owner to be cared for. The team members walked over to be with Doc, ignoring the freshly scrubbed kid beside him.

"Wish I could talk with Gutsy. I've some news for him," said Jeb.

"Just because I'm clean, doesn't mean I can't talk," said Gutsy.

Six startled men stared at the duded-up boy who spoke with Gutsy's voice.

"You be Gutsy?" shouted Flatnose.

"Who else would I be?" snapped Gutsy.

All six men laughed, slapping each other on the back.

"You look like a dude mule skinner going courting," shouted Petre.

"Got any more of those duds? I'd like me a set," Rocky said, or rather it was more like a howl.

"What's the matter? Do I look funny?" asked Gutsy, beginning to be unsure of himself.

"Naw, kid, you look great. You look like a real mule skinner. Soon as I can, I'm gonna get me a set of those duds, and we'll parade together," said Jeb. He laughed with the rest of the men.

"Not without the rest of us, you won't," said Cookie. "We'll make a fine sight, all of us duded like Gutsy. You better join us too, Doc, as we parade up and down Main Street.

"First, let's go to the mine office. The boss has something important to say to Gutsy," said Bible John.

"Yep, you've gone and made yourself a hero again, by gum! You're the doggonest, luckiest kid I've ever seen," exclaimed Cookie.

"Come on, let's get this over with. We've got to get all dudified so we can show Cerrillos some real men," said Flatnose, grinning from ear to ear, making his flattened nose even flatter.

Gutsy, Jeb, Flatnose, Bible John, Cookie, Petre, Rocky, and Doc walked down dusty Santa Fe Avenue, followed by most of the townsfolk. Everyone turned right on Ortiz Avenue and headed for the Supervisor's office of the Ortiz Mountain Gold Mines.

Cliff, still a little breathless from the three-hour, fruitless ride, came outside to greet Gutsy and the growing crowd.

"Jeb tells me you're a fine mule skinner—a first rate Indian man and a pretty good saddler," began the Boss.

Gutsy swallowed and looked surprised at the list of his accomplishments as told by Jeb.

"I want to welcome you to Cerrillos, a land people have said is without law or order. But they won't be able to say that after today, now we've got a real preaching preacher and a medical doctor. We want to make our town a family town, and we hope you make it your home."

Cliff swallowed and continued. "Today you did us a fine deed. We're grateful to you; not only do we have our gold, but both miners are back with us. Jeb tells me it's by your help we have this caravan of tools and goods. The Ortiz Mines would like to show our appreciation to our newest mule skinner, present you with a fifty-dollar reward for bringing back the gold, and offer you a job as Jeb's helper on the next trip to Westport, the wages being the same as any other muleskinner's, excepting Jeb's, of course."

The crowd started to cheer.

"Wait, folks! Wait! There's one more thing. Gutsy, we'd like you to bring your family back with you, and I promise your paw a job in the mines when he gets here," said Boss.

The people cheered again.

"Folks, wait. You can celebrate in just a minute," said Boss, holding up his hand. "During the time you're on your trip, the mine will have a house built for you, so your family will be coming to a new home. This time, Jeb and you'll be guiding wagons back, as well as mules, so your family will be able to travel in a wagon. Now, one last word—welcome to the land of enchantment. You're the kind of people that will make this country even greater."

"Yowee!" yelled Gutsy. "Are we all going back?"

"Everyone who wants to," assured Jeb.

"When do we start?" asked Doc.

"How about now?" asked Gutsy. "I'm ready to go."

Seated at the very back of Barnes Saddle shop in Westport, Missouri, was Gustoferson Stevens, known to all as Gosi. His tall, scrawny body was crammed behind a stack of freshly stained leather, partly hiding him as he worked, expertly stretching one piece after another of aromatic, newly dyed leather over wooden saddle frames.

This day, March 16, 1824, he punched holes in the hides before using the strength in his permanently stained hands to pull the thongs through to lace the leather into place. Because his head was bent over his work, the sparkle in his wide-awake, brown eyes was hidden by his long blond hair.

The sparkle and the hushed breath were not caused by interest in his work, but by the conversation between Jeb Malonie, the newly arrived mule skinner, and Mr. Barnes, owner of the saddle shop where fourteen-year-old Gosi was indentured. He was meant to serve five more years at the grand wage of room and board and twelve cents a month.

Whenever a traveling man came into the shop, Gosi always eavesdropped. Jeb's stories, told in his inimitable drawl, were the best of any he had heard. Gosi was careful to not make any disturbance that would interrupt the smooth flow of conversation.

Jeb told of driving forty of the finest mules up and down the Santa Fe Trail, carrying freight one way and gold ore the other. He told of the new tools he would take to Cerrillos to help the miners in their search for precious metals. He mentioned the fine silks and muslins he carried for the wealthy women, wives or friends of the miners who had already found their strikes. He told of the good wages received by everyone in the area. His excitement at being a part of this newest gold rush was contagious, exciting each person who heard him.

Gosi could see himself as part of the returning freight train, riding at the side of Jeb, helping drive the train that carried the cargo to the mines of Cerrillos. The idea of adventure beyond the confines of this unrewarding job led him to speculation—his favorite activity, a mental game of "What If."

Why, he thought, *if he were with Jeb, he might even see the famed Indian chief, El Dorado, who, legend said, was so rich that each morning his tribesmen painted him with gold and each evening washed it away.* Gosi imagined how it would be if he, Gosi, could have the right to empty the bath water—just once.

With just one tub of gold-filled water he could pay off old Barnes and be free. One thing for sure, when he was free, he would be like Jeb, running a mule freight train, trading, swapping exciting tales, and learning about the entire western part of his country.

Gosi leaned forward a little too far in his eagerness to hear better and knocked over a stack of leather. As Gosi's luck would have it, this stack was next to a rickety table with an oil wick lamp resting on its dusty surface. The oil spilled, splattering several pieces of finished leather, staining them.

Confusion reigned. Leather slid every which way, and the odor of the tanning solution, combined with dye, rose from the dislodged stack and permeated the air.

Old Barnes yelled, "It's that clumsy, worthless Gosi. This piece of business will get him fifteen lashes."

Gosi shuddered. His back ached from yesterday's whipping and the one from the day before. He was sure old Barnes would have to aim very carefully in order to put fifteen more lashes on his back without repeating a spot.

Like a frightened pup, he fled out the back door, past the barn where he slept, deep into the forest. He ran and ran and ran for hours, his thudding feet sounding, to his ears, like an elephant herd in the otherwise quiet woods. He was much deeper in the forest than he had ever been. He came upon a small stream. Gasping for breath, he fell to the ground and drank deeply of the cool, refreshing water.

He rested, listening for sounds of people or galloping horses. His belly told him his breakfast had not been enough to satisfy his longing for lunch, too. The position of the sun in the sky told him it was nearer to supper time. Looking around, he saw some berries on the banks of the stream. Eagerly he picked handfuls for his supper. He decided it was time to stop and think about this latest problem.

No doubt about it, if old Barnes caught him, not only would he lose his skimpy bowls of soup for supper for months, but his wages also. He would be whipped many more times than the usual fifteen lashes. Old Barnes always declared piously that it was his responsibility to train the boys to make good saddles and to help them learn their true place in life.

Gosi knew that his term of indenture would be extended. Old Barnes said the law gave the master that right. He said the boys were just beginning to earn their keep when their seven years were finished, and Gosi knew he would use this latest episode to add months—or years.

The more Gosi remembered his past, the more determined he was to change his future. The stories of good wages at the gold mines gave him courage. It was obvious to Gosi that his solution lay in the freight train, in following it to the work near the mines in Cerrillos.

He was sure he could live on very little money and save the rest to buy his contract from old Barnes. This was important because his drunken father had agreed that if Gosi failed, his younger brother, Herman, would fulfill the contract with the saddler.

The decision to go to the mines was perfect. According to Jeb, gold was first discovered on the Ortiz Mountains by a shepherd who had picked up a rock to throw at his sheep and realized it was heavier than others. He examined it closely and saw flakes of gold throughout the rock. Maybe he, Gosi, would be lucky and pick up a few rocks and buy his freedom. The future settled, Gosi turned to more immediate problems.

Most important was his lack of knowledge of which direction the freight train lay. The next consideration was clothing. He had only what he was wearing, and even if he found a place to buy more, he had no money. His one pair of handmade shoes were of good saddle leather scraps, but they would not last long on a rough and extended eight-hundred-mile hike over the Santa Fe Trail. Food could be found as he traveled along. He knew how to trap animals, and he knew he could walk or run as quickly as the mule train, especially one of forty mule's length. The question still remained as to where he could find the train.

He walked slowly along the stream, stretching his tired muscles and thinking. He found a small, unoccupied cave in the side of a hill near the river bank. He felt his luck was holding, he would be protected for the night; and, he was sure to find the train the next day.

The cave was warm. He really did not need a blanket—at least not yet. Gosi thought of the morning when it would be chilly; he decided he would run then to keep himself warm. Snuggling a little farther into the cave, Gosi was happy. Things were promising. He burrowed even farther in, pushing the dried, wind-blown leaves underneath himself as a makeshift mattress, which seemed no worse than the one he had left behind.

This was better than being back in the barn at old Barnes Saddle Shop. Maybe his dreams of riches would come true sooner than even he had hoped—certainly faster than he could manage if he remained a saddler, especially a mediocre one as old Barnes had told him he would be. With these reassuring thoughts, Gosi dropped off and slept through the rest of the afternoon and the entire night.

He was awakened by the chirping of birds, the chattering of squirrels, and the brightness of the morning sun as it sent its exploring rays into the small, warm cave. Gosi dreaded to step out into the chill and frost of the mid-March morning, but he needed to stretch and unkink his legs and back. He was also very hungry and thirsty. Gosi tried to decide if he were more hungry than thirsty or more thirsty than hungry. Listening to the chattering squirrels, he knew he had the answer to his hunger.

He untangled himself and went first to the stream for a drink of water. He lay prone on the ground and scooped water into his mouth until he was no longer thirsty, then he crept silently to where the squirrels were playing. Quickly, they scattered to their home. Gosi followed. At the roots of a huge hickory tree, he found one of their caches of nuts. He removed some as he talked to the fussing squirrels.

"Friends, if you'll share some of your food with me, I'd be obliged. Won't even hurt your babies, nor try to capture you, though if I had a pot, you'd make a good stew. Berries are fine, but not enough to fill my belly, so I'll thank you for your help."

He filled both pockets of his leather britches and carried away as many nuts as possible in his hands. He returned to his warm cave. Gosi divided the nuts into three piles: one for breakfast, another for noon, and the last one for supper.